CHEYENNE GALLOWS

Digging gold in Sonora they had outsmarted the claim-jumpers. Now they aimed to buy the biggest Texan horse ranch this side of the Great Divide. But they stopped at Buckeye, and Nolan met Abby Lightfoot — half-blooded Sioux, and full-blooded woman . . . Then the big trouble started. It would end hundreds of miles north, where Custer's shadow still lurked and hatred for the white man was part of life. Guns had started the feud and guns would finish it.

Books by Tyler Hatch
in the Linford Western Library:

A LAND TO DIE FOR
BUCKSKIN GIRL
DEATHWATCH TRAIL
LONG SHOT
VIGILANTE MARSHAL
FIVE GRAVES WEST
BIG BAD RIVER

TYLER HATCH

CHEYENNE GALLOWS

Complete and Unabridged

LINFORD
Leicester

First published in Great Britain in 2005 by
Robert Hale Limited
London

First Linford Edition
published 2006
by arrangement with
Robert Hale Limited
London

British Library CIP Data

Hatch, Tyler
    Cheyenne gallows.—Large print ed.—
Linford western library
1. Western stories
2. Large type books
I. Title
823.9'14 [F]

ISBN 1–84617–549–6

Published by
F. A. Thorpe (Publishing)
Anstey, Leicestershire

Set by Words & Graphics Ltd.
Anstey, Leicestershire
Printed and bound in Great Britain by
T. J. International Ltd., Padstow, Cornwall

This book is printed on acid-free paper

1

Old Pards, New Pards

When Bob Geary came into the saloon for his nightly poker-game, he paused, one hand holding half the batwings ajar as he squinted through the haze of smoke.

There was plenty of noise from the drinkers but that didn't bother him. What bothered him was the group of men gathered around the corner table at the rear under a fog of tobacco smoke, all intent on the game, holding cards, buying cards, throwing away cards.

Trouble was, the dealer was sitting in Geary's chair.

Light that had managed to penetrate the fog glinted dully from tousled fair hair showing under the pushed-back hat, threw hard planes of shadow across a narrow, square-jawed face further smudged by a few day's stubble. Geary swore softly under his breath, straightened the front of his middling-clean frock-coat and went forward.

He was the houseman and part of his job was to keep the drinkers happy and be friendly so they would come back again and spend their money. But on the short — or, what seemed to him, long — walk to the poker-table, he ignored every greeting. His gaze was fixed on the fair-haired dealer who cracked some sort of joke and had all the regulars chuckling by the time Geary materialized out of the smoke.

Some of the players glanced up and greeted him.

'You're late, Bob,' added one. 'Wondered if you were comin'.'

The fair-haired man lifted cool blue eyes and locked with Geary. The two men stared at each other and one by one the card-players looked up and awkwardly shifted their gazes from one man to the other.

Silence fluttered and fell over the

table like a moth singed by a candle flame.

Barnes, the storekeeper, spoke up.

'Oh, Bob, this feller asked if he could sit in. Name's Matthews.'

'Might be,' Geary said in such a low voice that the men weren't sure just what he did say. But the man called Matthews heard and smiled with a friendly nod.

'You must be Bob Geary. They been talking about you. Figured you must've got delayed by some feminine wiles.'

Geary didn't crack a smile or move his steady gaze.

'Not when my regular poker-group's waiting — and someone else is sitting in my chair.'

Matthews looked down at the battered old straight-back he was sitting in and then gestured to a vacant chair at the next table. The smile was still there, softening his hard face a little.

'There's one. Drag 'er up and you can sit in soon's we finish this hand . . . ' He looked around at the other players who seemed a mite wary now, as if sensing trouble here. 'We all set, gents? Or someone want to change their cards?'

'Mister, I don't want that heap of kindlin'. I want my regular chair. *And you're sitting in it!*'

'Aw, Bob, it don't matter that much,' said Shorty Connor, the local livery man. 'Here, you take mine and I'll get the other so's we can — '

'Sit down, Shorty. I want my regular chair.' Geary's face was chiselled granite. He wasn't bad-looking but there was something in his eyes that made a lot of men hesitate if it looked as though an argument could blow up. 'You gonna move, Matthews?'

Matthews sighed. 'OK, let's not have any trouble. We'll just finish this hand and then — '

'No, goddamnit! You finish nothing! You get outta that chair — *now!*'

'Hey, Bob!' exclaimed the startled Barnes. 'C'mon, man! This is a friendly game and — '

'The game's fine,' cut in Geary, teeth gritted, eyes boring into Matthews. 'It's him that's the problem.'

Barnes arched his eyebrows.

'Well, I dunno about that right now, Bob. You're — '

'It's reasonable, what Matthews said,' spoke up Casey, the Wells Fargo agent. 'Let's get this hand finished and then we can all settle down. I'll buy the first round.'

Geary reached across the man, grabbed Matthews by the shoulder and dug in his fingers.

'You gonna move?'

Matthews lifted his cool gaze and set down his hand of cards, face down, without looking.

'Looks like I better.'

He came up off the chair like an uncoiling diamond-back, one hand knocking Geary's arm aside, the other looping over and cracking against the gambler's jaw.

Men scattered as Geary stumbled, sprawled across Casey and floundered so that both men and the chair fell in a heap on the floor. By now the players had leapt to their feet and were shouting and drinkers came surging across, yelling, 'Fight! Fight!'

By then Matthews was standing with fists cocked and ready as Bob Geary clambered to his feet, face angry — also red and lopsided-looking. His eyes blazed and his teeth were bared as he charged in, upending the table into Matthews. The man was fast — he jumped to one side, but the heavy deal table-edge caught his hip and he staggered. Geary came in just as swiftly, fists swinging. He connected with two blows, one on Matthews' shoulder and the other on the side of his neck.

The fair-haired man stumbled and Geary came striding in, lifted a knee. Matthews spun aside, but Geary's outer thigh caught him, knocking him off balance. He dropped to one knee as Geary lunged, kicking. Matthews punched the leg on the calf-muscle, knocking the limb violently aside and spinning the gambler. As Geary tottered, trying to keep his balance, Matthews rose off the floor almost languidly and stabbed two straight lefts into the houseman's face, snapping his head back on his neck. A right looped across and spread his nose all over his face, blood spraying. Bob Geary gulped as blood filled his throat, then Matthews shifted his attack to the man's midriff, arms going like pistons, driving Bob back step by step.

Geary hit a table and scattered the drinkers there as he rolled across and took the table to the floor with him. When Matthews stepped around it the gambler came up swinging a chair. It whistled past the fair-haired man's face and the legs splintered. Faster than a blinking eye, Geary thrust the jagged edges at Matthews as he rushed in.

Matthews grunted as the splinters pierced his trail shirt and broke off in the ridged flesh over his lower ribs. He backed up as the jagged wood ripped the cloth, caught, then stabbed him again. This time he jumped back. Geary lunged and stumbled. Matthews clubbed a fist down on to the other's forearm, Geary released his grip and the chair swung wildly as he tried to hold it with the other hand. Matthews kicked it out of his grasp, stepped up close, taking Geary by surprise. He rammed his head down, the forehead cracking across Geary's already busted nose. The man howled and turned, stumbling, then righted and actually ran crouching through the roaring spectators to the bar, hands covering his bloody face.

Matthews hurled two tables aside and strode purposefully after the gambler, reached him and twisted a grip on to the man's frock-coat. He hauled back and Geary came around, swinging instinctively. Matthews fended the awkward blows easily, then drove the same fist into Geary's face.

The knuckles skidded off in the film of blood but the blow was solid enough to twist the houseman's head violently.

He fell against the bar, snatched up a bottle and hurled it.

Matthews ducked and by that time Geary was facing him with the jagged neck of a bottle held in his blood-covered right hand. He snarled an epithet as he lunged one leg forward like a swordsman trying to run his opponent through.

Matthews leapt back as the jagged glass slashed air less than an inch from his belly.

He stopped, frowned puzzledly at Geary, and warily started to circle away, crouching, watching that broken bottle. Geary stalked him, then suddenly he did a strange thing.

He stopped, looked down at the weapon in his hand and abruptly hurled it back across the bar as if he couldn't get rid of it fast enough. The weapon crashed on to a shelf of liquor, causing the barkeeps to duck as the tumbling bottles shattered and spilled expensive liquor.

Matthews almost smiled as he went

to meet Geary who was striding in now as if he would walk clear through a wall if it came between him and the fair-haired drifter.

They met with a dull thud of muscular bodies and the meat-cleaver sounds of fists hammering flesh. They grunted as they exchanged blows. Both men were sagging a little when there was the roar of a shotgun and a rain of dusty wooden laths and plaster flakes fell about them.

Panting, swaying, bloody, they blinked and turned to face the batwings. Sheriff Barney Wales, big, solid as a tree, ugly as a bull buffalo facing down a challenger at mating-time, cocked the hammer on the second barrel of the Ithaca shotgun he now used to cover the two fighters.

'Call it a draw,' he boomed, menacing with the riot gun. Both men could see by his eyes that he was itching for them to make more trouble; this lawman was out for blood and he had a couple of ready-made targets right in front of him.

He looked disappointed when both men raised their swollen, bloody fists with the split knuckles.

A single jerk of the Ithaca's barrels was enough to get both men lurching through the batwings on their way to the jail.

★　★　★

'How about that sheriff?' slurred Matthews, dabbing at his split lips and a cut over one eye.

They were in separate cells with only a floor-to-ceiling set of bars between them. Geary, sitting on the edge of his bunk, looked up slowly, bloody kerchief coming away reluctantly from his busted nose.

'Yeah. New broom. Barney's a hardcase,' he said after a pause, voice hoarse. 'They say he rode the owl-hoot trail a few years back, took a job as lawman and destroyed every Wanted dodger he could find that had his name or picture on it. He was ready to blast us — *wanted* us to give him trouble.'

Geary grunted, not in the mood for conversation. But the other man said quietly: 'Broken bottles are something new for you, aren't they.'

Bob Geary stared hard for a long minute, his left eye closing rapidly as blood and fluid filled the bruised lid.

'Sorry about that. You damn well riled me, bustin' my nose that way! Never expected to see you again. Thought you were tucked away safely in jail.'

'Time off for good behaviour.'

'*You*! That'll be the day!'

Matthews walked across to the bars, his battered face unsmiling as he looked down at Geary still sitting on the bunk.

'Where is she, Bob?'

Geary glanced up slowly. He sighed heavily, stood slowly and walked across, one-eyed gaze steady on Matthews' battered face. He looked hard and long.

'Matt, I hear she's somewhere north of Cheyenne, on a big spread out of town. Has an interest in it. Could even

12

own it for all I know.'

Matt Nolan's jaw dropped. 'Get away!'

'True. As far as I can find out, anyway.'

'Where the hell did she get the money to . . . Aw, Christ! No! You didn't . . . ?'

Geary nodded sadly.

'Look, Matt, I was mighty damn weary from searching and I had my own troubles. Maybe I *let* myself be conned — I ain't sure. All I know is her and Wolf denied taking the gold and I guess I was ready to believe 'em, so I could get on with my own life. I'm sorry, Matt, but I just didn't have it in me to keep going as hard as I had been.'

'Son of a *bitch*!' swore Nolan quietly. 'And you left her there?' Nolan sounded belligerent. 'Up in Wyoming, enjoying our gold!'

'Matt, she's prosperous enough to hire herself a couple of fast guns for protection. And I mean fast! Old enemies of ours: Bodine and McAlpine. Some say the law's in her pocket, too — if not her bed.' He paused but Nolan's face didn't change expression. 'I looked into it, Matt, but I can't pin anything down. Not from a distance — and I had to make a living. So I figured I'd best leave things be.'

'You sure loused it up good, didn't you.'

Geary bristled. 'You knew what she was like! You shoulda warned me!'

'I *trusted* you, that's what I did! Trusted you to look after my wife when I got railroaded into Yuma . . . ' Nolan stopped abruptly, eyes narrowing. 'You have a hand in that?'

Geary swore an oath. 'Just as well they got these bars between us or I'd rip your goddamn head off for that!'

Nolan's gaze held a few moments longer, then he nodded

'Must've been her and the old man. Thought they might've needed some help. Ah, a man's a fool!'

'Huh! Told myself that more'n a

14

thousand times over the past coupla years . . . ' He suddenly spread his arms. 'Well, that's about it, anyway, I guess.'

'You give up damn easy!'

'Look, Matt, I'm doing all right where I am as houseman. It's a reasonable living, not too dangerous, not too many hassles. Unless old pards show up on the prod!'

'You were the one insisted on that goddamn chair. Hell, Bob, we thought we were gonna be the richest cattlemen and horse-breeders in Texas!'

Geary grimaced, clapping the cloth over his nose as it started flooding again. His voice was muffled.

'Dreams! Hell, we got the money together all right, busted our backs digging gold in the Sonora rush. Then you married that squaw. That's when our troubles started!'

'She's not a squaw. Part Sioux is what she is.' Nolan looked ready to bend the bars if Geary gave him an argument on that score.

'Well, her old man's a full-blood and so was that half-brother. Look, forget it, Matt. We had our chance and we lost out. You can't get near her. But we can start again, just the two of us. If you want, that is . . . ?'

'Been a few changes since I saw you last, Bob,' Nolan said quietly, firmly.

The flat tone stopped Geary in his tracks. He frowned.

'Like — what?'

'Like I shared a cell with Amos Cline for a spell.'

'I heard they strung him up.'

'They did — and I never want to see another hanging. I'll take a bullet when my time comes. Anyway, Amos was a queer cuss, knew he was gallows bait, wanted to pass on his 'secret' of fast drawing. Wanted to leave something to the world, the way he put it. Made me practice in the cell at night, even carved me a wooden gun, and when I got out — well, I've been a long time getting here. Practised plenty.' He paused, then added: 'And put it to use a couple times.'

'What? Gunfights?'

Nolan nodded. 'Hear about Notch Blaine in Abilene?'

'Hell, yeah. They say his gun was only half-way clear of leather when a feller no one'd ever heard of, named Travis, nailed him dead centre. *Hell*! Travis is your middle name!'

'Used it for a spell. Matt Travis.'

'I don't believe it! You were never a gunfighter!'

'You been listening to me?'

Slowly Geary nodded. 'By God! You — you saying you could go up against Bodine and McAlpine?'

'And win,' Nolan said flatly.

'Judas, boasting was never like you, either!'

'Just stating a fact, Bob. I don't go hunting trouble. But if it's there, I don't aim to dodge it.'

'No, you never did. Say, reckon we could try?' He was beginning to like the idea now. 'I mean, I'm still riled as hell at the way she conned me. And I've always felt bad about your side of it. We pards again?'

They shook hands through the bars, but Nolan held on to Geary's hand and looked steadily into his face.

'One thing — we don't get the money from her, *you* owe me my half-share.'

Geary scowled. 'Yeah. You've changed, all right!'

2

Long Trail Awinding

Barney Wales hauled rein and pointed to the haze-blurred hills slightly to his right.

'There she is — the county line.'

Nolan and Geary, both showing bruises and swellings from their fight, glanced at the hills, then at each other. Wales watched, his big ugly face impassive. But he drew their attention to the shotgun he carried across his thighs by drumming his fingers against the breech — just in front of the hammers.

'I got a clear view from here, boys. All the way to the top. I aim to sit here till I see you two go over that crest.' His voice hardened. 'If you've got any sense at all, you won't try to outsmart me by doublin' back. Just keep on goin' to

19

Cheyenne — and give my county a wide berth from now on.'

He leaned forward a little in the saddle, leather creaking with the shift of weight, dum-dum eyes raking the two dishevelled men.

'I see either of you this side of them hills again, you'll be nothin' but a bloody smear on the trail when I ride away.' He patted the shotgun again, then bared big, yellow tombstone teeth in a tight, mirthless smile. '*Adios*, gents. Ain't that what you Texicans say?'

'I could say a little more,' Nolan allowed but didn't. The sheriff jerked his head.

'Ride!'

So they rode. To the foothills, then, after a glance back that showed them Wales still sitting his big brown gelding with the painted rump, watching them, they began the long climb to the top.

By the time they reached the crest, both men and their mounts sweating, they were ready for a rest.

Sheriff Barney Wales was still there

below. But now he held a Winchester rifle instead of the shotgun. They found that out not so much by sight, but by the fact that the lawman threw the weapon to his shoulder and they heard the slapping echoes of two shots an instant before the bullets laid silver-grey streaks across the sandstone boulders just below where they sat their blowing mounts.

'That's damn good shooting!' allowed Geary.

Nolan said nothing, wearily kicked his heels into his claybank's damp flanks and set the horse on the last few yards of trail that would take him over the crest. Geary followed and they rode on down the far side a good twenty yards before stopping on an unexpected grassy bench. They dismounted and allowed the horses to browse while they sat on a log and rolled cigarettes, using Nolan's tobacco sack.

'Wales lied,' Geary said, getting Nolan's attention. 'His county line's further north.'

Nolan tensed. 'What's he playing at?'

Geary shrugged. Their smokes were half-finished when Nolan said: 'How did Wales know we were headed for Cheyenne?'

Geary looked up sharply. 'Not sure that he did. It's just the biggest town in this direction.'

'A lot of towns in between — but he said 'go to Cheyenne' like he knew that was where we were headed.'

'What you getting at?'

'He could've heard us talking in the cell — we heard him in his front office chewing-out some townsman. The words came down the passage like they were in the next cell to us.'

'Yeah. But Barney talks like a broadside of cannon anyway. We weren't talking loud.'

Nolan was dubious. 'We were both on our bunks — mine at the far side of my cell. We were talking pretty loud.'

Geary seemed puzzled. 'So what? No skin off Barney Wales's nose whether we go to Cheyenne — or Laramie or

Billings, Montana, for the matter of that.'

Nolan looked at him steadily.

'We mentioned a heap of gold we'd dug outta Sonora — '

'Aw, hell, Wales is new here but he's got it sweet. Runs the town the way he wants, collects a few dues here and there — a little percentage from the gaming tables, a cut from the cathouses, dollar a head for every drunk he gets off the streets, and a lot more.' Bob Geary shook his head. 'Wales ain't been here long but he's a big frog in this pond and he likes it that way. We don't have to worry about him.'

'He was quick enough to kick us outta town. Hell, he couldn't rightly say I was a fiddlefoot on the bum, and you had a steady job. He *wanted* us outta town. Bound for Cheyenne.'

Geary stubbed out his cigarette against the log, watching Nolan carefully. He saw the fair-haired man's wide shoulders tense.

'You never used to be so suspicious.'

Nolan's tough face showed no softening.

'Well, look what trusting folk got me. You want to try a couple of years in Yuma. You take things at face value in there and you stand a good chance of fertilizing the warden's flower-garden.'

Geary frowned, blinking. 'What's that mean?'

'From six feet under.'

Bob Geary's mouth sagged slightly. 'Get away! You mean he buries — men? In his garden?'

'So word has it. Man dies in there, no matter what the cause, warden's special burial squad takes him away and no one knows where. Got the biggest, brightest flowers you've ever seen.'

'What? No graveyard? Not even a marker?'

Nolan shook his head.

Geary blew out his cheeks. 'Well, hell almighty! That ain't right! A man's last resting-place should be marked!'

'Well, the warden's is. They carved him a tombstone outta gen-u-ine marble.'

'He — died?'

'Big rock rolled on him during one of his visits to the quarry. Just as well. There was no chance of remission for good behaviour while he lived.'

'His dyin' was — lucky for you, eh?'

'Yeah. I'd been in long enough to qualify for remission. Applied for it. He gave me seven days solitary in the oven — five-by-five iron box in the middle of the compound. Bread and water every second day. If they remember.'

'Hell, Matt. I never knew it was so bad.'

'Time in the oven was a picnic to some of the things that son of a bitch could think up.'

'That — boulder that crushed him . . . fall by itself?'

'Little mystery there. Would've taken six men to move that rock. Even then they would've busted their backs, or cracked their muscles.' He rubbed gently at his right shoulder, deadpan. 'Dunno what happened, really.'

Bob smiled slowly. 'You have five friends in that place . . . ?'

'We were all friends that day. Could've called on five dozen if they'd been needed.'

Nolan stood, still rubbing at his shoulder, swinging the arm the way a man does to ease pain when he's strained a muscle that is slow to heal.

'Let's get down outta these hills. Wouldn't put it past that Wales to come and hurry us along with a couple of shots.'

They rode down slowly off the bench. 'I give you my word, Matt,' Bob said quietly, 'I had nothing to do with sending you to jail.'

'You'd be dead by now if I thought otherwise.'

Geary frowned deeply. Once again he was startled — and maybe just a mite scared — at the way those years in prison had changed his old pard.

★ ★ ★

First place they came to had a saloon-cum-store with built-in whore-house above, and three or four cur dogs roaming the rutted street and alleys. It was little more than a trading post with a few outbuildings, a trashheap on the trail.

It must have had a name but they never learned it. The drink was poison and the grub not much better. The prices were through the roof, but before they paid Nolan grabbed Bob's hand when he made to reach into his pocket for the money the barkeep-owner asked for.

'We don't have that kinda money,' Nolan told the barkeep and the man's dirt-caked face began to harden.

'You come into my place, order and eat my grub, then tell me you can't pay?'

There were shadows moving back of the bar at one end, just beyond the reach of the watery lamplight.

'Didn't say we *couldn't* pay,' Nolan informed the big man who was stooping a little so he could reach beneath the bar. 'Only said we don't have that much money between us.'

The saloon man flicked his stony gaze from Nolan to Geary.

'Your pard was reachin' for his poke.'

'No — he was reaching for his gun,' Nolan said easily and saw the surprise flicker over Bob's face before the man locked his features into hard lines. 'This is Lash Kinnane. Just killed a man south of the range. We got out ahead of Barney Wales's bullets but only just. Had to leave our stake on the table.' He lowered his voice. 'Some damn hawkeye spotted Lash's mark on the ace of spades.'

Geary stiffened but went along with Nolan, scowling at him.

'Why din' you bring that army bugler we met along the trail? He coulda got everyone's attention, made sure they heard you!'

The trader straightened slowly and the moving shadows shuffled to a halt.

'You met an army troop?'

'More like a company,' Nolan said tightly. 'Few miles back. Thought they was after us but only wanted to know if they were on the right trail to this dump. Talk of moonshine and hideouts for men on the dodge, long as they can pay. Said they're gonna put an end to such shenanigans.'

The barkeep was leery. 'You two on the dodge?'

'Not from the army, only Barney Wales,' Geary said. 'I figure we've paid for our meal and your hospitality by warnin' you, mister.' He turned to Nolan. 'We'd better hightail it or we'll be caught in the massacre.'

'Massacre!' croaked the unwashed man.

'Shoot! Sorry, just slipped out. Ah, you better know, I guess. Heard the captain talkin' to his lieutenant. They aim to wipe you off the map. Said you've been here too long. They're totin' a Gatling gun on wheels,' Geary added flatly. 'Take our advice and hightail it pronto, friend.'

There was a lot of sudden movement in the gloomy saloon and in no time at all Nolan and Geary found themselves out on what passed for the street. Their mounts were weary and no one was paying any attention to the tethered horses at the hitch rails.

So, when the pair cleared town, laughing, they each had a fresh horse and a full belly, even if the greasy meal didn't sit as quietly as they would've liked.

Once past the wooden arched bridge over the creek they slowed. Geary came in close alongside and punched Nolan lightly on the shoulder.

'Easy! That's the one I strained in the quarry! Taking a helluva long time to heal.'

'Sorry. Hey, how about that, eh? Nearly three years since we seen each other and we slid like a couple greased hogs right back into that old razzin' routine . . . '

'Nothing like a guilty conscience to start imagining all kinds of things when the army's s'posed to be closing in.' Nolan let loose a brief, loud laugh. 'Damn! First laugh I've enjoyed in a coon's age! Maybe things're looking up for us!'

'Could be. If she ain't spent all the gold, that is. And if you're as good with a gun as you say.'

'You'll see for yourself when we find her — and Bodie and McAlpine. Or should I say 'if' . . . ?'

Geary sobered. 'Only know what I heard. I can't guarantee nothing, Matt. She might not even be in Cheyenne.'

'Then if you're wrong you still owe me a heap of *dinero, amigo*.'

Geary stiffened, jerked towards Nolan's dark shape beside him.

'By Godfrey — I b'lieve you mean that!'

'Keep on believing it, Bob. Someone's gotta pay for those years of hell . . . and I don't care who.'

Geary bit down on the whiplash retort that sprang to his lips.

This was the second time that Matt

Nolan had sent a shaft of numbing fear through him.

And he didn't like it one damn bit.

★   ★   ★

The men from the trading post had no sense of humour. They didn't see the joke, being buzzed by the threat of a non-existent raid by a couple of smart-ass drifters.

Geary hadn't even considered that they might get really riled and come after them. But Nolan trusted no one these days and he was the one to spot the three riders picking a way through the timber.

He said nothing right away, just dropped back a little and half-hipped in the saddle to keep an eye on the trio.

'How long you been houseman in that saloon?' he asked suddenly and Geary looked mildly surprised as he swivelled to answer.

'Nigh on nine months — was due for

a bigger piece of the action till you showed.'

'Blame Wales, not me. You have any cause to shoot your way outta trouble?'

Geary frowned. 'Gambling trouble?' He shook his head firmly. 'I was on a good deal and likely the most honest card-man south of Deadwood.'

'You ain't forgot how to use a gun, have you? Pistol or rifle?'

Geary felt the tension knotting within him now.

'No,' he answered slowly, 'I ain't forgot. Why?'

Nolan jerked his head downhill.

'That trader and his pards can't take a joke, it seems.'

Geary swore, unsheathing his rifle. Nolan already had his across his thighs and was levering a shell into the breech.

'They're the ones we're meant to see. Could be more up ahead waiting for us to ride into an ambush while them three hold our attention.'

Geary nodded and smiled wryly.

'That suspicious nature you've developed might just be working for us after all.'

Nolan was studying the country up above on the steepening slope.

'We're gonna have to slow down where the trail zigzags below that bunch of boulders,' he said slowly, thinking it through. 'Be sitting ducks for anyone up there waiting to draw a bead on us.'

Bob Geary agreed that the boulder clump was the most likely place for bushwhackers to be holed up.

'Those three below are closing in fast!'

'Pushing us. Don't let 'em faze you! You spur ahead now, you'll hit that hairpin too fast, be dead meat before you can slip the saddle. Which is what they want.'

'Hell! We ride slow and they can take their time at sighting in on us!'

'Rock and a hard place. We've been in a hundred of 'em. Or don't you remember?'

Geary didn't care for the mocking

34

edge to Nolan's tone and his own words were clipped when he snapped:

'You seem to be running things, Sergeant. What you suggest?'

'Keep moving just as we are, making for the zigzag.'

'And get ourselves picked off!'

'But we don't turn into the zigzag. We go straight ahead, swing up through that patch of brush.'

'Christ, Matt! It's riding blind! That brush is all intertwined — got more damn knots than a fishin' net! We dunno what it's hiding!'

'Could be a deadfall or two, some broken rock that'll make our mounts stumble. But it's just as likely to be ground no more rugged than we're riding over. And once in there, we're on the same level as the boulders, maybe even slightly above . . . '

Geary knew he was out of practice at this kind of thing. He ran a tongue around dry lips and drew down a deep breath. He swallowed.

'OK! You always were Custer's

favourite scout because you showed initiative. Let's go!'

The three men below started shooting, coming on at a jerky pace, their bullets kicking dirt all over the countryside. Nolan and Geary feigned surprise, made for the zigzag trail. Out of the corners of their eyes they saw sun glint from two rifle barrels up in the boulders.

Nolan had been right: the three below were there simply to push them into the ambush.

Geary followed Matt Nolan's lead as the man made as if to turn into the zigzag trail. He saw one of the ambushers lift a little for a better shot. Then Nolan's rifle came up smooth and fast to his shoulder and cracked once. The bushwhacker jarred backwards, rifle flying from his grip, and the second man got such a shock that he jumped up into full view to see how badly his pard was hit.

He never found out because Nolan's next bullet took him between the shoulders and kicked him off his rock to disappear from sight. By then they were plunging into the brush and they wheeled their mounts to face the three men who were supposed to be creating a diversion.

Suddenly, the trio found themselves targets and they weren't really ready for it. They scattered, shooting wildly, and Geary and Nolan, now screened by the brush, hammered shot after shot at them, sunlight flashing from spinning, ejected cartridge cases. A horse went down and its rider yelled as he sailed into the slope with bone-shaking impact, lay there, writhing, a leg snapped between knee and ankle.

One of the others slammed sideways out of the saddle, hit the slope and kept on going down, sliding and spinning, raising his own dust storm. The third man yanked his horse down-slope but made the move too quickly. The horse stumbled and he fell two-thirds of the way out of leather, clinging desperately to the reins and bridle as the panicked animal laid back its ears and plunged down the grade. It would take a ship's anchor to stop it before it hit the flats way below and the rider would likely be down in the dirt long before then.

The hillside was hazed with gun-smoke and dust, noisy with the yells of the man with the broken leg, the whinny of frightened horses, the clatter of sliding rocks as the runaway kept going.

Geary stood in stirrups to get a better view, but when he looked back at Nolan he saw that the man was already pushing fresh loads into the smoking rifle's magazine. A little sheepishly he sat back and began to reload his own gun.

Two men were dead, one wounded, and another had a broken leg. The fifth man was either still clinging desperately to his bolting horse or was down somewhere on the lower slopes.

Geary was surprised when Nolan made a splint for the one with the broken leg and bound up the chest wound on the gunshot man — who was the rancid-smelling barkeep from the unnamed trading post. His name was Marney.

'Din' 'spect you to — do this,' he gasped as Nolan knotted off the last strip of torn cloth he was using as a bandage.

Nolan grunted and saw Geary looking strangely at him. Obviously *he* hadn't expected this small show of humanity either.

'No sawbones out here,' Nolan said shortly and made for his horse. Geary moved slowly towards his own mount and knew that that was as much explanation as he was likely to get.

'You better not come — back through my — place!' gasped the trader as they started to ride up-slope again.

'That's OK,' Nolan called back. 'No need to thank me. I'd do the same for a cur dog.'

Geary pulled a wry smile. 'Likely you'd carry the dog across your saddle till it healed!'

'Yell yourself hoarse for a medic in Yuma and never see one,' Nolan said quietly. 'Everyone's gotta help everyone.'

It pleased Geary to see Nolan's discomfort: the man still had some of his old traits, even if he didn't want to admit to them. Bob Geary suddenly felt a whole lot easier about riding stirrup-to-stirrup with Matt Nolan now.

Prison had hardened him but it hadn't smothered all his good points, even if Nolan made out it had.

As they started away, the trader called after them.

'Hey! Heard you talkin' over your grub at my place. That squaw. She runs the Sioux Agency at Elk Mountain — nor'-west of — Laramie. In the Medicine Bow foothills.'

Nolan nodded. 'I know it. *Gracias, amigo.*'

The man fell back, coughing.

'Get outta here, you son of a bitch!'

3

Spit at the Devil

The man who had escaped from Nolan's and Geary's guns was named Cansdale. He had been reluctant to be involved in the ambush in the first place and when the two drifters turned out to be so deadly with their weapons, his one notion was to escape.

He was congratulating himself on having made it successfully when suddenly a rider appeared blocking the trail ahead. A big man on a brown gelding and holding a heavy-calibre rifle. Sunlight glinted off the brass star pinned to his ragged-edged vest.

'In a hurry, Cansdale?'

The sweating ambusher reined down fast, his horse skidding with stiffened forelegs.

'Judas! Sheriff Wales!'

'What's set your ass on fire?'

Cansdale swallowed. He was not a man long on guts and he had tangled with Barney Wales on occasion in the army. They weren't encounters he remembered with any pleasure. He ran a tongue around dry lips, jumped when he heard the rifle's hammer click back under Wales's thumb. The gun wasn't yet pointing at him but he saw by the sheriff's face that it would be — much too soon.

'A little trouble up-trail, Sarge — er — Sheriff,' Cansdale stammered, jerking a thumb over his shoulder.

'*Big* trouble is my guess. You ain't carryin' any guns that I can see. Just an empty holster and saddle scabbard.'

'Uh — lost 'em in my hurry to get away.'

Wales waited, big, coarse face set in hard, uncompromising lines. Cansdale squirmed.

'Them two fellers you threw in jail. They — they stopped by Marney's tradin' post. Sort of — tangled with him a little, made him look foolish. He got drunk an' riled after they went and made us go after 'em.'

'Us bein . . . ?'

'Well — usual bunch. Sully, Mac, Hugo an' me — well as Marney, o' course.'

'And as fine a bunch of back-shooters as ever assembled north of the Panhandle — go on.'

'They — they musta spotted us. Laid up for us near the zigzag.'

Wales snorted, hawked and spat. '*Who* laid up for *who*?'

Cansdale wasn't about to admit he had been part of a carefully laid ambush. He shrugged, ignored the question.

'Shot the hell out of us — '

'*That* I believe! Bunch of losers like you rats.'

'Well, it weren't funny! Sully an' Mac are dead. I think Hugo busted a leg an' Marney was shot outta the saddle. Might still be alive.'

43

'And you ran — stayin' in character, Cansdale.'

'Well, hell! That Nolan — he's a dead shot.'

Wales nodded shortly. 'Figured him to be — had that gunfighter look. Geary's no slouch either. Well, you better show me where it happened.'

Cansdale stiffened. 'I ain't goin' back there!'

The rifle barrel swung down and lined up on his quivering body.

'Turn your hoss around and start ridin'. I can find the place myself if I have to.'

Cansdale found enough courage to scoff.

'You wouldn't shoot me! It'd be — murder!'

Wales flicked his eyes side to side.

'Don't see no witnesses. Anyway, if you turn up dead Nolan and Geary'll get the blame.'

Cansdale's bladder was on the verge of voiding as he fought his mount around on the narrow trail and started it back the way he had come.

Wales kneed his own horse forward, keeping the rifle trained on the shaky ambusher.

*   *   *

The trail north to Cheyenne was long and arduous and, as demonstrated at the zigzag, not without risk.

'I've come a long way since I left Yuma,' Nolan said as they passed through a deep-shadowed ravine. 'Covered a lot of country looking for you, Bob — and her.'

Bob Geary glanced up sharply.

'Look, Matt. You gotta get it clear, we still can't be sure she's where that trader said — but seems to fit in with what I heard. Sort of.'

'And you never followed through!' Geary shrugged and Nolan's voice hardened. 'Couldn't't've been looking all that hard, Bob.'

'Judas priest, Matt! I'd been trying to find her for *years*! Like you, I figured she or the old man had had you railroaded to jail. I was good and mad. I mean, half that gold was mine and they'd run out with the lot.'

Nolan smiled wryly. 'And here I thought you were after their hides because they'd set me up . . . your old pard!'

Geary's mouth was tight, his face hard.

'I was plenty mad at what happened to you, Matt, but there wasn't anything I could do about it, except maybe try to get a good lawyer. But I'd've needed the damn gold for that!'

'OK, OK, don't get outta the saddle. But what stopped you tracking down the Cheyenne rumour?'

Geary was silent as they rode slowly across a trickling stream, the hoofs splashing slightly, echoing from the narrowing high walls. The sky above showed just as a ragged blade of blue.

'Well, there was nothing really solid to go on. But I'd been looking for her for so long that I automatically started

46

to follow through, and then I thought it was a damn long way to go, just on hearsay. I mean I didn't really figure she'd run so far.'

'You ought to have. That's where her people are, scattered right across that country. Custer found that out.'

Geary nodded. 'Well, I'd been searching for a long time. I was damn weary of the whole deal, needed cash, whether I went or not. Then, I fell into that dealer's job.'

'What's that mean, 'fell into it'?'

Bob Geary hesitated. 'Well, I sat in on a game with Ace Wells, the houseman. I saw him stacking the pack and, like a fool, said so out loud. He was mighty touchy as you'd expect. I guess I was on a short fuse, too. I was losing.'

'You nailed him?'

'Only just. Son of a bitch had one of those arm rigs with a Sharps derringer up his coat-sleeve. Luckily it caught on a seam, gave me time to put a bullet into him.' He shrugged. 'Saloon owner

47

didn't seem to mind; put on an act to make it look as if he'd known nothing about Wells cheatin'. Then I said in front of everyone I could do a better and more honest job as houseman. Kinda put him on a spot and he said, 'OK — show me'.'

Nolan watched him closely.

'You were never no slack with a gun. You sure that Sharps caught on a thread?'

Geary smiled crookedly.

'We-ell. Sounds better when I tell it that way. More like self-defence on my part — like I had no choice but to shoot first. Wouldn't want anyone to think I accused him wrongly . . . ' He grinned wryly. 'I needed a job bad, Matt.'

Nolan laughed. 'You always had a sly streak in you, Bob! So, you found yourself a job and that kept you from going after Abby, huh?'

They had cleared the ravine now, but when they saw how low the sun was in the west they turned back and decided to camp by the trickling stream for the night. They were spreading their bed-rolls before Geary answered.

'The job paid well enough. I kicked in a small percentage to the saloon. Seems that crooked dealer was not much liked round town anyway, and suddenly a lot of folk began smiling at me and saying 'howdy' on the street. I got cheap meals at the local diner, my hoss stabled for free, smiles and winks from the saloon gals and — sometimes — a little more'n smiles and winks. Hell, I was *happy*!'

'I get it. You found a pretty good life and figured why bust a gut trying to find Abby and maybe run into a bullet. I mean, I was out of the way, in jail . . . '

Geary looked uncomfortable.

'Well, I guess that's what it came down to. I had me a little tussle at night, trying to sleep, knowing you were there in that hellhole, but convinced myself there was nothing I could do anyway . . . '

Nolan had the fire going now, began slicing sowbelly while the skillet heated and the grease sizzled and spattered. He said nothing and Geary frowned.

'Matt . . . ? I did feel bad, real bad.'

'Sure.'

'Dammit, I did! I hit the booze for a spell, nearly lost my job, but pulled myself together. Then I find you sitting in my chair, dealing a hand like you'd taken over — just like you used to when we were pards! The old sarge throwin' his weight around! Just wandered in and expected to be boss man again. It made me mad!'

Nolan used his knife-point to flip over some of the slices of sizzling bacon, looking up at Geary from under his hatbrim.

'If I took over anything, anytime, it was because I saw it as the best thing to do at that moment. You had a tongue, could've said if you didn't like it.'

Geary dragged down a deep breath as he prepared the coffee-pot, filled it with stream water. He nodded slowly.

'Yeah. Well, you know I mostly keep things to myself. But you were right: most times it was the best thing to do, you taking over. It riled me just the same.'

Geary said no more and Nolan concentrated on his cooking.

In Yuma there had been plenty of time to think about a lot of things. One thing which had bugged him for a long while was that the few times when they'd been riding together he had caught Geary looking at him as if the man wanted to kill him.

He thought now that he had the answer to that — but he hadn't suspected that Bob had resented his leading before. And, despite himself, he wondered just what else he might have missed in those reckless years when they had thundered through the frontier together, laughing, carousing, spitting in the face of the devil, as if there was no tomorrow.

Matt Nolan wondered for the thousandth time just who had railroaded him into Yuma Penitentiary — and why?

★　★　★

Well, 'why' was easily enough answered, he told himself after they had rolled up in their blankets and he was smoking one last cigarette before settling down to sleep. Yeah — someone wanted that gold and saw a chance to put him out of the way.

That left two people who knew about the gold: Abby and Bob Geary. She might have told her father, Wolf, though . . .

As the months crawled by while he was in jail, he'd told himself Geary would never betray him that way. But a man suffering pain and humiliation every day, with no change in the foreseeable future — well, he could get some mighty strange notions . . .

Geary and Abby. There had been moments when he thought about them inside the depressing stone walls: moments which, he decided, might have meant more than had appeared at the time. Abby was a strange woman,

independent, fiercely proud, coura-
geous, beautiful — all qualities that had
attracted Nolan to her in the first place.

Could they also have attracted
Geary . . . ?

Squirming now in his blankets he lay
on his back looking up at the stars,
remembering how it had happened . . .

Sonora had been a hell of a place, a
back-busting, muscle-cracking black
purgatory that had shortened their lives
by much more than the eight months
they had worked their claim — and
come out with a small fortune.

What with claim-jumpers and plain
murderers all over the place, it hadn't
been easy to get their gold out. Once
they had struck the seam that led to the
mother lode they had had to curb their
desire to whoop it out loud and shout
their success to the skies. They had
man-high piles of gold-bearing quartz
to hide.

For once it was suspected that
payable gold had been located by any of
the miners, the shadow men would

hone their knives and prime their pistols — and pretty soon the successful miners would mysteriously disappear from the diggings, or their mutilated bodies would be found in some dry creekbed — runaway bucks from the nearby Painted Rock reservation usually got the blame. Then cold-eyed strangers moved in on the claim . . .

So Nolan and Geary made a plan. Outwardly, they struggled to locate a few odd nuggets — pocket-money only — but at night, the apparently disheartened pair returned to their mineshaft and worked the seam. It was mighty hard, too, because noise had to be kept to a minimum; the only light was a candle that burned with a dull glow in the foul air. Then the overburden that had been removed had to be scattered about the tunnel so that it blended in with the other useless rock and general debris on the floor.

This took most of the night; sometimes, while they were working on a rich section of the seam, damp, grey daylight would creep in and eventually swamp the candle's pitiful glow. They would have to return hurriedly to their camp — only yards away but in plain view — and go through the pretence of having just woken up, ready for the day's grind.

'Today's the day, boys!' old Pop Gander would say as he hobbled past with his wooden barrow. (He said it every day.) 'Can feel it in me bones!'

''Luck, Pop!' Nolan or Geary would call back.

He would amble off, knowing his years would prevent him from ever reaching a rich seam unless it was only bare inches below the surface. Other miners exchanged ribald remarks or good-natured banter, still others ignored everyone on their way to their claims, and Nolan and Geary, worn out from their night work, would try to look cheerful and energetic as they stumbled into their own mine.

One would keep watch while the other snatched a little sleep. Then they would swap roles so that when darkness came and they shuffled back to their camp, dirty, shoulders slumped in outward disappointment, they were really eager to start swinging picks and shovels and using hammer and chisel and pry bar.

It was mighty hard on them but they made it.

Not that they fooled everyone. They worked the seam until it petered out, closed out the claim and prepared to set off for parts unknown. They had stashed their gold in the timber on the slopes above the diggings, bit by bit, using part of their night hours to do this. They had laboriously cracked the quartz, crumbling it so that the gold, in nuggets and thin seams, worked free. Then they scattered the rubble.

This way, they unearthed the claim's riches and loaded the heavy gold on to the two burros, dumping the tools they no longer needed, and started off again.

Then four of the hardcases who preyed on lone miners and jumped claims suddenly appeared out of some trailside rocks. There was enough sunlight here to glint off the guns they held. Nolan and Geary didn't hesitate.

They swung across the slope, then down. Nolan, by previous arrangement, tossed his burro's halter to Geary as he swerved into some rocks. He was quitting saddle, rifle in hand, before the horse even came to a halt.

The bandits came in fast, shooting, but their bullets were wild because the two miners were moving so fast and were so well co-ordinated in their movements: long ago they had worked out what actions to take should they be jumped.

Nolan's rifle cracked like a string of fireworks and two of the killers pitched out of their saddles without a sound. The horse of a third staggered and stumbled and the man swayed wildly in leather. The action saved his life as a bullet whipped the hat from his head. The fourth man had a shotgun and he got off one barrel as he veered back towards the rocks which had hidden him and his companions. Geary brought up his rifle and triggered. The slug kicked the hatless man out of leather and he hit the slope awkwardly, rolling down, dust raising.

Geary fired into the screening, roiling cloud but the wounded man came out of it, on his belly, shooting. His bullet grazed Geary's neck, snapping his head back as he lurched from the saddle. He grabbed wildly at the horn. His hand closed on it and he hung there, his rifle's foresight snagged on brush. As he fought to free it, the wounded killer struggled to one knee, beaded quickly.

But as his finger curled around the trigger Nolan shot him in the head. The man slammed down flat on his back. The shotgunner had quit leather now, brought the heavy weapon around. Once again the floundering Geary was the target but when the killer saw Nolan spurring up-slope, he shifted aim.

Nolan gripped his empty rifle in his left hand and swept up his Colt from its holster in a smooth motion that surprised himself, firing the instant it came into line with the target.

The killer's shotgun blasted, but the barrel was pointed to the ground and the man crumpled, spilled raggedly down the slope . . .

Those four weren't the only ones to try for the hard-won gold.

Sharp-eyed, unscrupulous men noted the sag and strain on the *alforjas* packs on the burros and tried their luck. Most learned quickly that their luck had run out. Others decided to give Nolan and Geary a wide berth as they made their way through the Sierra Nevadas, heading for Arizona, aiming to swing north into Utah, or maybe turn south and east towards Texas.

Things went pretty much according to plan until they hit a town called Buckeye, about half-way between the Gila Bend mountain range and Phoenix.

There was a travelling theatrical troupe in town and the boys figured they could afford to take time to unwind and celebrate a little. A few drinks, maybe some female company.

This they did but Nolan was astonished to realize the he had been smitten by the Indian girl who appeared in the theatre company's stage show at the Rialto, a maid of the wilderness, sleek and golden-skinned with hair like the wing of a raven.

He cut loose with a whoop and a holler, grabbed the startled Geary and swung him around.

'Hey, man! You see that? She *smiled* at me! Huh? How *'bout* that!'

'You see those two braves siding her in her act?' Bob Geary warned. 'The older one's ready to kill any white man who looks at her sidelong. And I think he's already holding back the young 'un.'

But by this time Nolan had a lot of redeye inside him and he threw caution to the winds.

'Hell, I'll sweet-talk 'em around, toss 'em a nugget or two — we can afford it — and save my best sweet-talk for that l'il beauty!'

'You're plumb loco! You won't get within spittin' distance!'

'Hey, I aim to get a lot closer'n *that*!' And, displaying the reckless charm he had often used before, Nolan set out to woo the beautiful Indian maiden.

No one was more surprised than Geary — unless it was Nolan himself — when within three days the couple were married by a preacher whose qualifications were admittedly suspect, but there was a ceremony of sorts and the older Indian seemed content enough, the younger brave as impassive as his wooden counterpart standing outside the general store down the street, advertising tobacco and cigars.

Her stage-name was Abigail Light-foot, and she became Abby Nolan, showing those brilliant white teeth in a flashing smile that reflected in the warmth of her dark eyes.

'Hope you know what you're doing, Matt,' Geary said quietly and Nolan surprised him with his reply.

'I love her, Bob! Just hit me outta the blue when I saw her standing on that fake rock on stage amongst them fake trees. I'd give her anything in the world.'

'Not my half of the gold!' Geary lightened the remark with a laugh. 'Only joshing — but what d'we do now? When we started out we didn't plan on anything like this.'

Nolan grinned sheepishly.

'We don't need to change our plans. We can still get that horse ranch in Texas. Just means building an extra room on the cabin.'

They were easy-going times and Geary shrugged and agreed.

'Sure, why the hell not? Be someone to do the cooking anyway.' Soberly he asked: 'What about the old man and the buck?'

'Heading north. I gave 'em a little gold for expenses. Be just the three of us going to Texas.'

Geary seemed relieved at that. But

— uncertain, too.

Then, before they reached Texas, before they even crossed the Arizona line into New Mexico, trouble came out of nowhere.

4

Jail-bound

The old Indian was called Black Wolf on stage, but his real name, his Sioux name, was Shunkaha. He said very little but his eyes held contempt for the whites and their strange way of life, even if he did earn a kind of living from them.

It puzzled Nolan when he realized how little Shunkaha thought of white folk. Once he asked him about it.

'How come you look like you wouldn't spit on us if we were on fire, Wolf,' giving him the name he was best known by, 'yet you work for us?'

'Close to Fawn,' he said, 'Fawn' being part of Abby's Indian name.

'You . . . worried about her?'

The cold eyes were answer enough.

'Whites are what I worry about.'

Nolan nodded. 'You let me marry her.'

'You are white, yes, but I — sense — some Indian ways in you, No-lan. Good ways. Few whites have impressed me like you.'

That surprised the hell out of Nolan, but he didn't accept it on face value. There was something about Black Wolf that bothered Nolan: the man's eyes contained only a little less contempt when he looked at Nolan than when he settled his gaze on any other white man, including Geary. Only a little less — the other Indian, Horse, showed open hatred for all whites, Nolan in particular. The only time his eyes softened was when he looked at Abby.

'Your father sure hates whites,' he ventured one night when he and Abby sat alone outside the camp, Geary in his bedroll already. She was silhouetted against the stars, fine-chiselled features lit by silver.

'My mother, brother and sister were killed by Custer before Little Big Horn.

Shunkaha survived and has felt guilty ever since. He can never forget — his hatred is very strong.'

For some reason the words sent a chill through Nolan.

'But Custer's massacres happened years ago — and Wolf's living in our towns now. A long way from his stamping-ground.'

'Because he watches over me, with Horse Catcher.' He was her half-brother, a man slightly older than Abby, sober, taciturn, well-muscled, reticent, rarely speaking to anyone. It was clear he worshipped Abby, his half-sister.

Nolan decided not to worry about it. He could savvy Shunkaha wanting to make sure his daughter didn't fall foul of every lecherous white man who set eyes on her — and plenty did during the trio's stage act. It was mostly a series of tableaux with painted backgrounds, stylized glimpses of Indian life, including some on-stage archery, chanting and posturing by Black Wolf as he 'communicated' with the Great

Spirit, and breath-catching glimpses of golden skin during poses by Abby. Horse Catcher would be a formidable foe to come up against, defending her, but Nolan felt the old man would be the most dangerous: he held so much hate within, disguising it.

Anyway, they seemed to have accepted him and he figured to just let things flow. When Wolf and Horse Catcher said that now the act was broken up they would head back to their own country, Nolan was relieved. Naturally enough, Abby was sad and there were long days when she would not speak to him — or Geary — but isolated herself. Nolan let her come round gradually and soon things settled back to something like normal.

They said their farewells to Shunkaha and Horse Catcher, the latter's eyes lingering long on Abby and longer, steadier, still on Nolan.

'You watch — treat her good, No-lan.' That was all he said but there was a lot more implied: not the least being the casual way he placed his hand on the hilt of his hunting-knife in its beaded buckskin sheath at his belt.

The old man gripped Nolan's fore-arm in the Indian way, held it, staring deeply into the white man's eyes. 'I trust you, white man. Do not make me sorry for doing this.'

Nolan didn't figure there was much use in crossing his heart or making any kind of oath that he would look after the girl, so he merely nodded, and still Black Wolf lingered with his grip on his arm. Then the Indian nodded jerkily and released him.

'You good white man: only one I know.'

The strange thing was, neither Indian said any kind of farewell to Abby. At least none that Nolan saw.

The trio, Abby, Nolan and Geary, moved out of town the next morning. The other Indians were nowhere in sight so they started out into the sunrise that painted the desert country with colours no artist would use in a picture for fear of being accused of exaggerating nature.

Then, a few days later, they came to a lawless frontier town called Featherstone Creek. Nolan and Geary didn't want the girl in that depraved, wide-open town, so they set her up in a secure camp by a bend of the narrow, sluggish creek under some cottonwoods. Completely at her ease and unafraid, she said she would bake them some corn dodgers and biscuits. The two ex-miners rode in to town to replenish their supplies, aiming to be back by mid-afternoon.

But when it came time to leave town, Geary, who had taken on a load of liquor, much more than Nolan, refused to budge. He looked over the shoulder of the faded redhead in his lap, squinting through some of her stringy hair, and grinned owlishly.

'Not that I don't enjoy your comp'ny, Matt, ol' pard,' he slurred, 'but there're certain things you can

— cannot supply.' He winked ponderously. 'Gemme?'

'Try to make it by sundown, Bob,' Nolan said, smiling as he shook his head and made his way out of the saloon and back to his horse.

He was surprised to see a man in the camp when he rounded the bend.

Even more surprised when he recognized Black Wolf. The Indian stood beside a tarp shelter that Abby had rigged earlier and, face like carved basalt, he gestured to where the woman lay on her buffalo robe, covered with a blanket, her torn buckskin dress off to one side.

Nolan was out of the saddle in a blurred movement, knelt beside Abby, saw her bruised and cut face.

'God almighty, what's happened here . . . ?'

There had been two of them, Abby told him, dry-eyed but sobs convulsing her battered body; drifters, who must have thought they had it made when they came upon her alone in the camp.

70

She heard only one name — 'Dutch' — spoken by the youngest one, she told Nolan as he tried to comfort her. It was just before the other grabbed her from behind and flung her to the ground, ripping the fringed buckskin dress from her lithe golden body. She had been punched in the face and body and it was obvious she must be in considerable pain.

'Did they . . . ?' Nolan was still coltish enough in his outlook on life at that time to hesitate over using the word 'rape'. Instead, he gestured awkwardly as she moved to huddle by the fire now, shivering, clutching the torn red blanket about her with one hand, the other nursing a tin mug of coffee prepared by the sombre Indian.

She looked straight into her husband's face.

'Only the older one,' she said in a firm voice. 'The young one was too — shy. He — couldn't . . . '

'That won't save him,' Nolan said standing, checking the loads in his sixgun.

Wolf stood there impassively, watching with approval in his eyes. Nolan frowned at him suddenly.

'What're you doing here?'

'I — sent for him,' Abby said and when he snapped his head around to look at her, she tapped her forehead. 'I have — missed him and Horse. I asked him to meet us somewhere along the trail . . . '

This didn't surprise Nolan so much: he had lived with Indians long enough to know it was possible for them to contact each other telepathically. But for now . . . He turned to Wolf.

'Glad you're here, Wolf. I'm going after these bastards.'

Wolf nodded slowly. 'I know. You will do well, Nolan.'

★   ★   ★

Nolan caught up with them in some rocks on a hogback rise, just the kind of camp someone with a guilty conscience would make so they could watch

72

approaches. He came in out of the darkness as they sat over supper, a fresh-killed jack rabbit spitted on a stick above the fire. He had heard the shot earlier. It had led him here — although, strangely, they hadn't seemed to have taken trouble to cover their trail.

One man was in his mid-forties, the other not much more than a kid, about twenty, Nolan figured. They stared apprehensively at him as he came in with his rifle braced into his hip.

'Whoa, there, wrangler!' the older one said, standing slowly, the half-cooked rabbit dripping fat from the spitstick he held down at his side. 'You're welcome to supper, but if you're lookin' for *dinero*, you're outa luck.'

'If you'd taken time to search our camp you might've found more gold than you'd ever dreamed of.'

They exchanged glances.

'Your camp?' said the kid.

Nolan nodded, face grim.

'The one where you found the Indian girl.'

Again they exchanged glances, the kid looking really worried. The older one, Dutch, spoke slowly, apprehensive now.

'That was your place, huh? Man, you oughtn't take a chance like that, leavin' that good-lookin' squaw out there alone! You never know who might — '

The rifle shot drowned the last of his words and Dutch cried out as he reeled, collapsed on his side, writhing, his right leg shot out from under him. The kid jumped back three feet, eyes wide, as Nolan levered a fresh shell into the breech. Dutch howled, looking up with pain-contorted face, propped on an elbow now.

'Jesus, man! What — what the hell you — doin'?'

The rifle crashed again and Dutch sobbed in pain as the lead smacked him down and his left arm dangled from a shattered shoulder. The kid made a choking sound, turned and began to run. Nolan shot him in the right hip and he fell, spilled back across the fire scattering the burning twigs. Most of the light went and Dutch worked his sixgun free of his holster. He triggered a wild shot at Nolan. The bullet clipped the outside of his left shoulder, spinning him.

But his rifle barrel came round and spat flame — and this time, death. Dutch's head snapped back as the lead took him between the eyes and he lay still except for a twitch or two from his legs.

The kid was crying.

'Don't! Please, don't! I — we — I never done nothin'! I swear!'

'Kid, you're about to learn too late that just being with some son of a bitch who rapes lone women and beats the hell outta them is the same in my book as taking part.'

The kid stopped crying, though he sniffled loudly, wiped mucus from his nostrils with the back of his hand.

'Mister — you — you got it wrong! We never — '

'Too late, kid. You wanna die just

lying there with a snotty nose or you gonna try for your gun like a man?'

Before Nolan had finished the kid's eyes bulged and he made an animal whining sound as he fumbled at his holster.

Nolan's rifle crashed, but the kid got off his shot even as a bullet took him down. His lead creased the side of Nolan's head and knocked him out for several minutes. Then it was another twenty minutes before he could see and walk properly, blood sliding down the side of his face and neck, staining his shirt collar.

He went through the mean-looking camp, found a couple of fresh biscuits and corn dodgers from the batch Abby had baked that morning. It was enough to satisfy him that they had been there all right.

He rode out. *Let the coyotes have them*. Men like that didn't deserve a decent burial.

★   ★   ★

When he got back to the camp there was no one there. Everything had gone except his warbag, the tarp, and some food. Bewildered, feeling the effects of the bullet crease, he looked around in the gathering darkness, but couldn't find tracks of any kind.

What the hell . . . ?

He threw up and shivered, knew that shock was setting in. The kid's bullet must have creased some nerve. The world spun crazily but somehow he managed to ground-hitch his mount and spread his blankets.

His body rolled on to them and he passed out.

★   ★   ★

Then, in the early hours, another visitor entered the camp. He was a big man with a droopy moustache, accompanied by two hard-eyed, gun-hung sidekicks. They ghosted in, waking Nolan roughly. The big one didn't beat about the bush, introduced himself as Marshal Ben

Tallack, from Pima County, his gun covering the bleary-eyed Nolan.

'Been trailin' a couple fellers half across Arizona.' His pale blue eyes turned frosty. 'Found 'em. Or what's left of 'em — just enough to show they'd been shot.'

Nolan blinked, mighty slow to wake up.

'Dutch Skene and a young feller called Chance Ohlrig — maybe a name you've heard?'

Nolan nodded slowly, yawning now.

'Heard of an Ohlrig, got a big spread north of Tucson. Not Chance though . . . '

'That's Starr. Chance was his kid brother. Starr sent him out with Dutch Skene, a frontier scout, to learn the ropes of wilderness livin'. They were s'pose to've checked in at Featherstone Creek but missed out. Know why, now.' He indicated Nolan's face with the dried blood. 'Cut yourself shavin', son?'

'It's a bullet-crease,' Nolan admitted heavily.

'Uh-huh. I gotta tell you, we back-trailed a hoss with a loose shoe to this here camp, startin' just a few yards from the bodies. You got anythin' to tell me, son?'

Nolan sighed. 'Guess I better . . . ' He told the Marshal about Abby being raped. 'Those men were the ones did it. Found some of Abby's fresh cooking in their grubsack.'

Tallack's face was impassive, unreadable.

'Well, I could savvy any man goin' after someone he believed raped his wife, ain't lawful, but I guess it's part of livin' out here.' Then Tallack's voice hardened. 'Only thing is . . . ' Tallack spread his hands, 'I ain't yet met your wife, mister . . . ' He looked around. 'Where is she?'

'I dunno. I left her here with her father in a state of shock. They're Santee Sioux, and they got their own ways of handling such things and communicating.'

'Now that's *mighty* convenient,' the

lawman said and his sneering deputies agreed with him. 'Where'd they go?'

'No idea. I was kinda woozy from this bullet crease and I . . . turned in. You woke me.'

Tallack spoke slowly.

'Like I said — convenient. No tracks showin' where they left — or were ever here!'

Gun hammers notched back and Nolan remained very still. 'I married Abby back in Buckeye. She was a showgal, at the Rialto with her father and half-brother — '

'That squaw?' broke in Tallack. 'You reckon you married *her*? Man, she hates whites! Her and her father both! And that damn brother! Jesus, the trouble they caused! Whites sniffin' around her, her kin tryin' to murder 'em . . . '

'Sounds like the whites caused the trouble.' But Nolan knew *he* was the one in trouble here. His thoughts were only just now starting to force their way through his throbbing headache.

No Abby, no Shunkaha, no tracks! *Everything was gone — including the gold!* But he didn't aim to mention that right now.

'We'd best have a word with this pard of yours you reckon is still in town. Geary, right?' Tallack turned to a deputy when Nolan nodded. 'Go fetch him, Luke.'

Nolan told the lawman his marriage certificate was in his saddle-bags. Tallack found it and laughed.

'Old Deacon McMurtry, huh? Man's a drunk!' He waved the paper. 'Might do to wipe your ass. But it could save your neck, too. Like I said, no one'd blame you for gunnin' down men who raped your *wife*. But this don't prove nothin', really. I think you'll hang. Judge Crane's a good friend of Starr Ohlrig's . . . '

But the judge who presided over the trial was not Crane, who'd been rushed to Phoenix with a burst stomach ulcer. Judge Cox had no love for Starr Ohlrig. His widowed sister had lost her land

and home when Ohlrig moved in on her river-bottom farm in a roughshod land-grab recently. Nolan's story hadn't been proved because he had been unable to produce his 'wife', who apparently had disappeared into thin air. Cox conceded Nolan had *believed* he was killing men who had raped her — evidence showed that this was the case — though Nolan had been drinking in town and alcohol might have clouded his thinking. In any case, Nolan had taken the law into his own hands and this was not acceptable. So . . .

'Five years hard labour, three if on exemplary behaviour.' Cox's gavel smashed into its wooden base as he glared at the cold-eyed Starr Ohlrig sitting amongst the public who had come to rubberneck. 'Next case!'

Geary was in the court room as Nolan was led past him on the way out. He was grey and hung-over, looked ashamed. His testimony had been bumbling, of no help. As Nolan passed him he said:

'Find her, Bob. Take care of her. I'll be back some time!'

'Not soon!' chuckled the deputy hurrying him along.

'You got my word, Matt! I'll look after her! I swear!'

5

Missing Gold

It was still dark in the ravine camp when Nolan heard Geary get up and relieve his bladder a few yards away against the sandstone wall. The man came back, sat on his bedroll and built a cigarette.

Nolan waited until it was burning and Bob had taken his first draw before speaking, startling his pard.

'You must've run into Abby somewhere along the line.'

'Hell! Don't do that! I thought you were asleep.'

'Learn to get along without much of that when you're in Yuma. Well? When did you catch up with Abby?'

Bob drew on his cigarette again, and tossed his tobacco sack and papers across to Nolan, who began to build a smoke as Geary spoke.

'It was Horse Catcher I came across first.'

That brought Nolan's head up fast but he said nothing, lit his completed cigarette from a dying camp-fire ember. Geary's voice had a faraway sound, as if he was there reliving the actual discovery . . .

'It was just after you were shipped out to Yuma penitentiary,' Geary began quietly, looking very sober now.

Bothered by the fact there were no tracks to show that Abby or Wolf had ever been at the campsite, Bob went back to check it again, without success, then left the vicinity of Featherstone Creek. He made a few tentative enquiries about Shunkaha and the woman in towns as he came to them. Nothing.

Once, after slaking his massive thirst with one too many whiskey-and-beer-chasers, he slipped up and hinted that there could be some gold involved. The barroom went suddenly quiet and it was enough to warn him to say no more. But — too late.

That night three intruders came into his lonely camp, guns drawn and knives ready to torture him. But Bob had realized he had been foolish even to hint at gold within the hearing of such men as lived in that lawless area and he was ready for them.

When he got the drop, they first tried to talk a deal, but it was only to hold his attention while one of them worked at getting out a hideaway gun. Bob was on edge, his heightened senses warning him, and as the gun came up, he fired, nailing the man in the chest.

They were experts at this kind of thing and while their companion was still falling the other two leapt away in opposite directions, one somersaulting to snatch up his weapon from where Geary had made him throw it. The other dived over a rock. Bob fired at the one going for the gun, missed, and the man twisted as he rolled up on to his shoulders, triggering. Geary lurched as lead gouged across his left hip, his leg buckling. He let himself go all the way down to one knee, fired again, hitting the man fatally this time.

Instinct saved him. He continued his rolling movement through and the bullet from the man coming up from behind the rock tore off his hat. Geary slid and spun, almost dropping his gun, and the killer jumped on top of the rock so as to get a clear shot at him, aiming down. Jerking on to his good side, Geary fired across his own body, gun barrel angled upwards. The killer screamed as the bullet went in just above his navel and tore up through his chest and major organs. He crumpled and by then Geary was running for his horse, a hand pressed into his bleeding hip, limping. *Maybe there were more than three . . .*

He reached his mount, spurred away, and a fourth gun, likely belonging to a man holding the horses for the other three, opened up. The gunfire was heavy, if wild, but it drove him up into the hills — just where he didn't want to go.

He had been told that renegade Indians were on the loose up there. Several white men had been found hacked to pieces after ignoring the warning. Geary glanced behind and thought he heard more than one horse following. Heart hammering, he rode wildly through the timber, climbing all the while. He still wasn't sure whether someone was following, but he wanted to get out of there as quickly as possible. He figured the best thing to do was to go up and over.

It was a sound enough idea, but by daylight he was completely lost, caught up in a series of brush-choked clefts between the hills and twisting ravines that led nowhere. He was also short of water and food, having abandoned his supplies back at his camp.

For two days he wandered, jumping at shadowy movements high up amongst some trees, certain-sure they were Indians. Then he found a trail that led him to a water-hole and he slaked his thirst. He felt better then, feeling he would make it out of here now.

But when he looked up he froze.

There was a naked Indian on a ledge, watching him. Geary's legs began to shake: being caught by renegade bucks in this kind of country was enough to give anyone the shakes.

Then he realized that the man hadn't moved, even though a bird landed on his head. It was a crow — and even as he watched, it took out the man's right eye with a few deft pecks. Grimacing, macabrely fascinated now, Bob drew his gun and climbed up there.

The left eye was already gone. And that wasn't all that was missing. The man's nose had been hacked off, his body mutilated so that Bob felt his gorge rise. He had also been partly scalped. But it was what he saw below the belt that finally brought the scalding bile spurting from Geary's mouth.

There was enough of the Indian left for him to identify Horse Catcher. He had been tied against the sandstone boulder where he sat now — for all eternity — and a fire had been built between his spread legs, feet staked. There wasn't a trace of genitals that could help determine the corpse's sex — even if it had been necessary to do so, which it wasn't.

It was a long time before Bob Geary settled down, his belly emptier than he could ever remember. He fled — that was the only word to describe the manner in which he left that ledge of horror.

Geary's words had stopped Nolan so effectively that his cigarette burned down and scorched his fingers and he didn't even notice.

'Horse Catcher? No mistake?'

'Man, there was just enough left to be sure. Christ, I can still see him! *Smell* him. That charred flesh . . . '

He shook his head sharply, spat, grimacing.

'That was real Injun torture,' Nolan said. 'Usually reserved for someone

90

who's committed some mighty serious crime forbidden to the tribe. They don't often treat their own kind that way, even so. What the hell had Horse Catcher got himself mixed up in?'

Geary shook his head. 'I don't think I'd want to know even if someone could tell me.' He cleared his throat. 'It was about six weeks later that I ran into Abby and Black Wolf — in New Mexico, just over the Divide, at El Centro. They were waiting for the stage to Socorro.'

* * *

Geary saw the small crowd that had gathered outside the stage depot. He realized most were townsfolk, looking at a smaller group of waiting passengers — and two figures amongst these who turned out to be Indians — Abby and Black Wolf.

One of the waiting stage passengers, a big, red-faced man with bright-yellow hair showing beneath his dirty brown derby hat, was thundering at the pair.

'Mister, I'm tellin' you, an Injun's got no right to expect to ride in a stagecoach with white folk!' The others growled and shouted. 'Now you back off before there's real trouble here!'

'Hell, he tried to pay in gold nuggets!' said the harassed stage clerk who was obviously on the side of the white passengers. 'I told 'im I wouldn't sell 'im tickets.' He nodded for emphasis, making sure the others knew where his sympathies lay. 'I mean, where would an Injun get gold anyways? Likely slit some white man's throat for it!'

'My gold is good,' the old Indian said. 'I dug it myself in Arizona.'

'Yeah? Where?' demanded the red-faced man. 'There's a helluva lot of silver in Arizona but not that much gold. Where'd you really get it? Murder some white man for it, I bet, just like the clerk said!'

The others growled agreement and then one of the passengers spoke up.

'I wouldn't mind if the woman rode in with us, but he'd have to ride in the luggage boot or up top.'

They looked at him, a pale, greasy-faced man with a small pencil moustache and a flashing smile: obviously what they called a 'masher' back East, a ladies' man. He got short shrift with this crowd, and while attention was diverted from them, Black Wolf and Abby edged away. She still had dark circles under her eyes and Geary noticed the way she moved: obviously, she was still feeling the effects of that beating she had taken. *All this time — some beating!*

Geary caught up with them as they made their way down behind the depot. When he called, they stopped, turned warily, Wolf dropping a hand to his hunting-knife. They recognized him but gave no greeting as he came up.

'You folk suddenly come into some money? Gold, I hear.' They didn't answer. 'I mean, trying to travel by stagecoach. Bit hopeful, weren't you?'

'We are very tired,' Abby said quietly. 'Our mounts gave out. We have come a long way, Bob. And I am — not well.'

'Heavy going, eh? Carrying all that gold, I mean? What'd you do? Bury it somewhere along the way?'

She frowned. 'Oh! You think we stole some of *your* gold! Yours and Matthew's!'

'No, I think you stole *all* of it!'

Black Wolf stepped forward, his knife half-drawn now. Geary drew his Colt.

'Don't tempt me, old man!'

Abby stepped past her father, getting between him and Geary, her eyes steady on the white man's face. 'We know nothing about your gold, Bob! My father came for me, and he took me away when Matthew left to go after the men who attacked me. We did not return. He had horses all ready for us, with our own food and necessities.'

Geary held her gaze. 'Then what happened to all the stuff that's missing from the camp? Most of our supplies, your horse, my new suit — the *gold*! You wiped out your tracks!'

94

She blinked. 'We know nothing about that! Perhaps someone came after us, found the gold where you and Matthew hid it while you went to town — '

'You knew where we stashed it! And how come your father tried to buy a stage ticket with gold nuggets? Where'd he get them, huh?'

'I work for them,' Black Wolf said quietly with a coldness touching the heavy tone he used. 'I think you and No-lan are hungry for gold. After she marry him, I go dig some. I think maybe I get enough to buy back my daughter from him.'

Geary blinked now. 'You — what? But you already gave 'em your blessing when they married, you lyin' old goat!'

The old Indian shook his head.

'I say only that if it is what Fawn wants, then so be it. I did not say it was what *I* wanted.'

Geary was puzzled. 'Then why didn't you just tell Nolan he couldn't marry her?'

'Because he knew I would run away

with Matthew, anyway,' Abby told him wearily. 'I was . . . smitten, at that time, acting foolish. I was not thinking . . . right. But by buying me back, Black Wolf believed I would see just how much he cared for me, needed me, that I would leave Matthew then and go back to him and the ways of the tribe.'

'And you damn well did!' Geary rubbed a hand across his forehead, shook his head slowly. 'Beats me the way you Injuns think. But it don't tell me what happened to the gold Matt and me worked for in Sonora.'

'Someone else must've taken it,' Abby said flatly.

Bob snorted. 'Look, I find it hard enough to figure why you ran off. You seemed happy enough with Matt. He treated you right, risked his neck goin' after them sonuvers who raped you, and landed in Yuma because of it! Then you pay him back by runnin' out and stealing our gold!' Geary stopped, said coldly: 'I'm beginning to think the whole damn thing was a set-up!'

'I know enough of your language to understand what you say,' Wolf snapped bleakly. 'You insult me! And Fawn!'

Geary started to reply but stopped, frowning now, looking from one to the other. He suddenly holstered his Colt.

'Well, that's just too bad you feel that way, Wolf. Looks to me like you ain't coming back to Matt, Abby. Just leavin' him flat!'

She had the grace to look embarrassed, dropped her gaze now. She shook her head briefly.

'My father needs me. I should never have gone against his will.'

'How about Horse Catcher?' Geary asked very quietly.

They both stared at him blankly, then she spoke.

'Horse Catcher makes his own way through life. He did not approve of my marrying Matthew. He knew that if he stayed he would kill him eventually and that would cause a rift between him and me, and the whites would hang him — so he chose to ride away

97

instead. He will come back one day.'

Bob Geary, remembering the horrifying figure he had found on the mountain slope, said nothing. Obviously, neither of them knew that Horse Catcher was dead and he didn't see any sense in telling them right now.

'You will keep looking for your gold?' Abby asked.

'Damn right. But mostly I was looking for you. Matt asked me to find you and take care of you until he gets out and I gave him my word I would.' His eyes and voice hardened. 'Now I dunno what the hell to do.'

'Keep looking for your gold, Bob,' she told him coolly. 'I know now how upset my father was that I married a white man. He dared not protest at the time, living among white men. He was afraid of what they would do to him. But I — I have seen the error I made and I understand it. Now I will go with him, and live the Indian life that we should never have left behind in the first place.'

Geary's jaw thrust out.

'Just like that, huh? A man's down, facing five years in that hell-hole, and you don't even flinch when you sink the boot into him?'

She didn't understand the allusion and he was too disgusted and sick of them both to explain. He started to back away, threw them a contemptuous salute.

'So long. Matt's better off without you, you ask me.'

'Tell him — I am — sorry — '

'Like hell I will! I don't savvy why you married him in the first place and I sure ain't about to add to his misery. Lady, you can go to hell, you and your old man both.'

As he strode away, Black Wolf called after him.

'Go look for your gold, white man! No good will come of it! But look anyway. Greed and murder are all any white man understands! Custer paid for his crimes; so will you one day!'

Geary didn't even bother turning his

head, strode back into the town, past the folk now piling into the stage which had arrived. He went into the nearest saloon.

'They flimflammed me, Matt,' Geary said heavily now, as grey light started to streak the sky over their camp in the ravine. 'I tried to follow 'em a day or so later but they gimme the slip, and I run into some of them renegades I'd been trying to dodge. They hunted me for more'n a week before I come across an Army troop. It was long after that I heard the rumour about her being up near Cheyenne, and I still figured you were better off without her . . . ' He shook his head slowly and sadly. 'I tried to find 'em again once but had no luck. I was broke, had to take jobs to live. Then I had a fall from a hoss I was breakin' for a ranch, laid me up for a couple months with a busted leg and I got snowed in come winter. I started out for Cheyenne again but got that job in the saloon and said to hell with it. I was plumb wore out from traipsing all over the country. I'd been doing it for two years, Matt, I figured that was long enough, that the goddamn gold was gone and we'd never see it again.'

He said this last while boring his gaze into Nolan: not challenging but laying it on the line, making it clear where he stood.

'You did your best, Bob.' Nolan rose stiffly from his rock and pressed his hands into the small of his back, arching it with a grunt. 'But I can't see who else could've taken the gold except Abby and Wolf. She knew where we stashed it.'

Geary nodded, started to rebuild the fire so they could brew coffee to fortify them against the morning chill.

Nolan sighed, shaking his head, mouth pulled tight.

'The whole blame thing, the wedding and so on, could've been just a set-up for them to get their hands on our gold. Bit of a long trail around, though, ain't it.'

'We-ell. Thought of that, too, and . . . there was the rape, Matt. They couldn't've arranged that . . . '

Nolan remained silent and Geary snapped his head up, frowning deeply.

'They couldn't, Matt! You saw the mess she was in, even days later in the court! Someone had really beat up on her, gouged her skin. Her clothes were ripped off.'

'I'm not letting 'em have that gold,' Nolan said flatly. 'We worked too damn hard for it. Sooner we get to Cheyenne or Elk Mountain and find out whether they're there the better.'

While Geary cooked breakfast, Matt cleaned his guns and reloaded both pistol and rifle.

There was a tight, bleak look about him that Geary had never seen before. With a shock, he realized he was looking at the face of a man ready to kill.

Eager — and impatient.

This Matthew Nolan was a total stranger to Bob Geary.

He wondered just what kind of hell Nolan had *really* gone through during his time in Yuma.

Whatever it was, it must've been pretty damn bad, to change him from the fun-loving, whoop-'er-up drifter he had been before meeting Abby Lightfoot, into this kind of murderous-looking ranny.

6

Cheyenne

They were well north on the Cheyenne trail when, one morning with the sun blazing down like a solid wall of heat as they rode around the base of a low mountain range, Bob Geary hipped in the saddle and spoke, his voice hoarse because they had been without water for more than twenty-four hours.

'That Starr Ohlrig. I was just thinking back to your trial. He looked mighty murderous when the judge put you in Yuma instead of stretching your neck.' He paused but Nolan merely waited for the rest. 'It's a wonder he didn't send someone after you. He's a man used to getting his own way. Fact is, I heard he had Judge Crane retired and later the judge had an accident that crippled him for the rest of his life. All because he wasn't there for your trial.'

'Heard about that in Yuma,' Nolan said quietly: it hurt to talk, he was so dry.

'And . . . ?' Geary was insistent, reluctant, as always, to let go of a thing until he had all the answers.

Nolan sighed, cleared his aching throat noisily.

'Ohlrig tried to have me killed in Yuma. First time on the rock-pile, Negro tried to spit me with a pry-bar, but I saw his shadow.'

'Judas! What happened?'

'He fell on the pry-bar himself. Took two days to die and admitted the word had gone out that Ohlrig would pay a thousand bucks and try to get parole for any man who nailed me.'

'Hell! There must've been plenty of takers in a place like Yuma!'

Nolan nodded, took his time replying.

'Things got a mite hazardous for a while. Couldn't use the latrine without some hopeful sneaking in and trying for me — or lying in wait.'

'How many tried?'

'Maybe six. I killed two. Broke another's arm. Pushed one off the quarry and gave him concussion for a week. He was never quite the same in the head afterwards . . . '

Geary pursed his lips: he was learning just what kind of hell Nolan had gone through in those years in Yuma. Yet Nolan was so matter-of-fact.

'How long'd this go on?'

'First couple of years. Once after that, but it might not have had anything to do with Ohlrig. I'd had a difficulty already with the feller who tried to bury me alive under a wall of dirt. Was him got buried. They let me alone after that. Believe some riled-up husband shot Starr . . . '

Bob Geary licked his cracked and raspy lips. 'Yeah — got too big for his boots. Or bed. No wonder you changed.'

'I'd be dead if I hadn't.' Nolan looked steadily at his pard. 'I'll never go back to that high-riding, spit-in-the-eye-of-the-devil ranny I was before I went to jail,

Bob. So don't go looking for that Matt Nolan. He died in Yuma a long time ago.'

'Well, I can savvy how it could happen, Matt, but don't be too damn bitter, pard! You're free now, you've served your time. We'll settle this trouble with Abby and Black Wolf . . . ' He tried to harden his voice, but his parched throat spoiled the effect he was aiming for. 'Or we won't. I mean, we could be all wrong, or something might happen to stop us. If it does, just accept it, Matt. There's more to life than getting square. Hell, few years back we'd've said to hell with it, got drunk, gone back to Sonora or some other gold-field and tried our luck again.'

'Like you say, Bob — a few years ago, yeah, we might've done that. But that would've been the old Matt Nolan. The one you're talking to now won't give up until this is all squared away and he gets his gold back. If you're smart, you won't even try to persuade him any different.'

Bob Geary, despite himself, felt a

cold shiver tingle down his spine at Nolan's words — and the look in those frosty eyes.

He merely nodded because he couldn't think of anything to say.

They found a water-hole just before sundown and drank their fill, splashed about in it, naked, horsing around. For a time Bob thought they had recovered that old reckless rake-hell kind of life they used to have. Then he noticed that Matt, while horsing around readily enough, never moved far from a flat rock a few feet from the bank.

His pistol rig was there, the cartridge belt wrapped about the holster, the Colt already loosened in the leather for a quick draw, should it be needed. He noticed, too, the scars on Nolan's torso and arms. He hadn't had them when they had run recklessly through the West. Looked like knife scars, or made by jagged, broken bottles. Once again he began to realize just how much of an ordeal Nolan had been through these past three years.

'What you got in mind once we find 'em?' Geary asked Matt as they ate a meagre supper while drying out by their camp-fire.

'Won't be able to work out the details till we see just what the deal is,' Nolan replied. 'But, in general, I guess we'll have to kill 'em.'

Geary jumped. 'Kill . . . Abby?'

'She's reverted to being Indian. You think she'll show us any mercy? You like to end up like Horse Catcher?'

'Aw, hell, Matt. I dunno about this. Kill a *woman*!'

Nolan looked at him across the rim of his battered coffee-mug.

'You don't have to tag along, Bob.'

'The hell I don't! Half that gold is mine, but she's likely spent it by now — or given it to the tribe or something. You figure that's right, she could be running the Indian Agency at Elk Mountain like Marney said?'

'Dunno why he'd say so if she doesn't.'

Geary pursed his lips and said

nothing more — he had plenty to think about.

Just as the slowly rising sun spread a watery light over the camp they awoke to birdsong and the distant snarling of a couple of spatting coyotes.

'Wake-up time!' Bob Geary said, ripping the blankets off the sleepy Nolan with a flourish. 'Come on!'

Naked, he ran into the water-hole, splashed his way out and sat down. 'Holy Joe! This's guaranteed to wake up a corpse!'

'If it's cold, I ain't interested,' Nolan growled hoarsely, groping for the blankets. Then he was swamped by chill water as Geary lay on his back, kicking wildly. He gasped and thought if he was getting wet and cold anyway, he might as well go all the way.

For several minutes they wrestled and splashed and ducked each other, just like the old days. Geary, gasping, half-drowned as Nolan dragged him to the surface by a handful of hair, spluttered and managed a grin.

'You got enough?' panted Nolan, grinning, too.

'Not by a long sight! This is too good to stop now!'

Geary launched himself at Nolan and once again they wrestled and tumbled about, hands slipping off wet flesh as they tried to push each other under. They were gasping and splashing and making a good din — but they heard the booming voice on shore clearly enough.

'Sure hope you two idiots ain't pissed in there. I gotta fill my canteens yet!'

They stopped instantly, breath blasting from their efforts, and saw the big man standing by their bedrolls.

It was Sheriff Barney Wales, and he had his sawn-off shotgun in one hand.

Keeping it pointed in their direction, he walked across and took their guns, then tossed them off to one side.

'Come on out, you murderin' scum!'

'What the hell . . . ?' slurred Geary, wading towards the bank, Nolan following more slowly.

111

'Get dressed. Slow and easy unless you want a leg — or worse — blowed off!' The shotgun's barrels menaced them, aimed at their lower bellies.

They dressed slowly. Wales watched, relaxed outwardly, but certainly tensed for instant action if necessary.

'What's going on, Barney?' asked Geary, buckling his trouser belt. 'Kind of outta your jurisdiction, ain't you?'

'My jurisdiction don't have any limits when I'm trackin' down a couple murderers.'

'We ain't murdered no one,' Geary said.

Barney Wales smiled coldly. 'Tell that to the five dead men you left near the zigzag trail, way back in Utah.'

'*Five*!' exclaimed Nolan. 'It was Tad Marney's bunch from the trading post. They laid for us and we nailed two, wounded two others and the fifth got away . . .'

'Now that's a pretty good story — 'cept I found the one you think got away. He'd been shot in the back.'

'We never backshot no one!' protested Geary but Wales ignored him.

'He lived long enough to tell me what happened. You made trouble at the tradin' post, waited along the trail and jumped 'em without warnin'. Way I found those bodies fits his story.'

'What the hell you playin' at, Barney?' Geary demanded angrily. 'That's not how it happened!'

'It's the way he's gonna say it happened, Bob. Don't waste your breath.' Nolan's cold eyes never left the sheriff's big, ugly face. 'Can't you see he's set it up this way? What you gonna do, Wales? Take us into Cheyenne, have the sheriff there toss us in jail?'

Wales continued to grin. 'That's exactly what I aim to do. I can get you tried there, too. They just finished building a brand-new permanent gallows, they been havin' so much trouble with lawless types slippin' across from Deadwood and the Dakotas lately. You boys just might christen that gallows!'

He chuckled, confident, pleased with himself.

Geary went white, looked sharply at Nolan but the man's face was unreadable, showed nothing.

'Or maybe we can come to some arrangement, huh?' Nolan suggested softly to Wales.

Geary was surprised to see the big sheriff's smile widen. 'Now that's a — possibility. Wonder why I never thought of that?'

'You got good hearing, ain't you?' Nolan said softly, puzzling Geary. Wales flicked an eyebrow and Nolan nodded. 'I thought so. That jail passage of yours carries sounds from the cells real good, don't it.'

Wales laughed. 'Feller who made it used to build churches in stone. He worked off some jail time doin' that cell-block for me. Said he used to make galleries so's the good folk could hear the preacher from every corner of the church. A right good mason, he was. You'd be surprised at the things I've heard from my front office, comin' outta those cells.'

'Might not be all true. Some men might say something to deliberately fool you.'

'It's been tried,' Wales said, hard-voiced. 'But I don't think *you* knew how that passage carried sound when you were talking about all that gold you and your pard worked at Sonora.'

Geary swore softly. 'So that's what brought you after us!'

Wales ignored him, watching Nolan.

'Think I'll let you stew a while first, so's when or *if* we get to dickerin' and hoss-tradin' you'll be in a better frame of mind and be reasonable. Sound fair?'

'Sounds just like the mind-workings of a damn shyster lawman to me,' Nolan said and Wales's smile disappeared.

He took one long step forward, rammed the shotgun into Nolan's midriff. Breath gusted and Nolan grunted as he staggered and fell to his knees. Wales slammed the heavy barrels across the side of his head and Nolan stretched out on the sand without a sound.

Geary froze, staring wide-eyed at the sudden eruption of violence. Slowly he looked at Wales, whose nostrils were flaring now.

'Barney, it was a couple years ago we got that gold! The squaw and her old man stole it. They'll have spent it by now.'

'Got a big ranch you told Nolan. Lotta money in there somewhere, and I aim to get a cut.' Wales grinned. 'Or mebbe the lot!' The sheriff spat and jerked his head at the unconscious Nolan. 'Get him draped over his hoss — and then we'll head on in to Cheyenne. I ever tell you my brother's the sheriff there?'

He roared with laughter at the look on Geary's face. Then he shoved the man roughly, ordering him to drag the unconscious Nolan across the campsite.

'Hurry it up. I wanna be in Cheyenne by noon.' He ran a tongue around his blubbery lips. 'Brother Monte's wife cooks a mean leg of pork, and I'm mighty hungry. *Move!*'

★   ★   ★

There was no roast pork for Nolan or Geary. They could smell it, all right, as it roasted and was basted in its juices by Barney Wales's sister-in-law in the sheriff's house attached to the Cheyenne jail.

Nolan was recovering on the bunk in his cell, ribs and belly sore, his head thundering, and a little curlicue of dried blood on his bruised face. He felt slightly ill and did not appreciate the saliva-producing odours of the roasting pork as much as did Geary in the adjoining cell.

There was a solid adobe wall between them. The only place where they could talk properly was down at the doors of their cells through the small, barred Judas windows.

'Matt. You OK?' Geary pressed his

face hard against the cold, rust-pitted iron bars in the window of his heavy wooden cell door. 'Pard . . . ?'

'I'm OK.' Nolan didn't raise his voice. If Bob couldn't hear him it was just too bad: his head was too sore to start yelling.

'You don't sound too good. You want something?'

'Why? They got room service here?' He heard Geary's chuckle.

'You're doing OK! That Monte don't seem a bad sort of cuss. Lot younger than Barney.'

Nolan had noticed but had nothing to say, Bob kept trying to engage him in conversation, gave up when he heard a snore coming from Nolan's cell. But if he thought Nolan had dropped off to sleep he was wrong.

Gingerly, grimacing and holding his head, Matt swung his legs over the side of his bunk, then climbed on top of the thin mattress with its worn blanket. He swayed, almost fell, but was tall enough to reach up and close his hands around the base of the bars in the high window.

It took some effort, but he gripped hard, tried to ignore the pain in his wrists where they rubbed against the stone window ledge, and pulled himself up far enough to see out. The rectangle of brilliant blue sky, washed by golden sunshine, had enticed him. Now he groaned, and dropped back with a dull thud to the mattress. He just saved himself from falling to the stone floor. Dizziness swept over him as he breathed hard from his efforts.

All he had seen was an enclosure of eight-feet-high fresh pine planks with a locked gate on the far side.

In the middle was the fresh-smelling yellow wood of a high structure that had only one use in this world: to speed some unlucky soul on its way to the next world — if one existed.

He had had a fine view of the brand new Cheyenne gallows.

It did nothing to settle his sore stomach or the angry throbbing in his head.

And it sure didn't help him sleep easy.

7

'Where Are They?'

'That was a right elegant meal, Lucille,' Barney Wales said, pushing back his chair, taking the stained table-napkin from his collar under his chin where he had tucked it before the meal. He belched and grinned, flicking his eyes from the woman to his brother. 'Pardon. But just goes to show I enjoyed it, huh?'

'I guess you could make room for a slice of my apple-pie?' asked Lucille Wales politely, a plain woman with a streak of grey in her hair and a warm face. And it was clear, to Monte anyway, that her expression concealed bare tolerance of the big sheriff from Utah. Long ago they had both become aware of the front that Barney Wales showed the world, while he kept hidden a much darker side. He'd even had trouble in the army.

Wales surprised them by holding up one of his big, blunt-fingered hands, shaking his head.

'I'd sure like some pie, but I guess I'll leave it till supper, Lucille. OK?'

'Of course.' She smiled and stood, beginning to clear away the dirty dishes. *Must have a belly-ache*, she thought. *I hope it's a big one!*

'How long you stayin'?' Monte asked; he was a good ten years younger than Barney, with a smaller, sharper face. He took after his mother whereas Barney had plenty of his big, brutal, ex-soldier father's genes surging through his system. Monte didn't sound too polite when he asked his question and Barney frowned, took out the makings and began building a cigarette.

'Well, young brother,' he put slight emphasis on the *young*. 'I ain't quite decided yet. Kinda depends a lot on them prisoners.' Suddenly he sat up straight as he saw Lucille taking the left-overs and scooping them on to two tin platters. 'What you doin' there, Lucille?' he asked sharply.

She brushed some dark-brown hair off her face and looked surprised. 'Why, making up lunch for the prisoners. I usually give 'em leftovers.'

'No, no, no,' Barney said; emphatically shaking his head. 'No, Lucille, these two don't deserve your fine cookin'. You give 'em some of yest'y's bread or biscuits and a little water. That'll hold 'em.'

Lucille glanced at her husband and Monte frowned.

'We feed our prisoners the same grub we eat ourselves, Barney,' he said. 'They're human bein's, you know.'

'Not this pair. They're murderin' scum, headed for the gallows.'

'All the more reason for them to have decent grub as long as they're in this life — '

'I said no!' Barney roared, making the woman jump. He looked hard at them both. 'These're my prisoners and they ain't gonna have no hotel-style livin' while I'm around.'

There was a challenge there and Lucille sighed. She began to scrape the food back into the big serving dish.

'Big brother,' Monte said flatly, letting Barney know he was aware of the man trying to use his family position to take charge here. 'Your prisoners — but in my jail, *and in my jurisdiction*! Now I recollect when you got me that deputy's job down south, long ago, just after you whipped me outta Deacon Perry's school, you beat my head more'n once because I went across the county line, outta our jurisdiction, chasin' law-breakers. You told me *always* to work within our boundaries — that way I'd never get my arrests thrown outta court and a tongue-lashin' or worse from some judge havin' a bad day with his ulcers.' He arched his eyebrows, watching Barney's big, coarse face tighten, hold, then loosen up considerably. 'You made me learn that lesson — and a hundred

123

others — which I ain't ever likely to forget. The big tough top sergeant runnin' folks' lives *his* way!'

Barney's eyes narrowed.

'You're toughenin' up, l'il brother, since I last saw you.'

'I like this here job, Barney. I follow the rules and I have no problems. I'll gladly keep your prisoners till you're ready to take 'em wherever you've a mind, but while they're here, you and them follow my rules, OK? An' that includes what they get to eat.'

Barney pursed his thick lips. He made a kind of neutral grunt, began building another cigarette.

'Was hopin' to have 'em tried up here in your court. Ain't no livin' witnesses to their bloody work, you see, just details I've uncovered durin' my investigations. Be more'n enough to hang 'em, though, an' don't see no sense in my havin' to drag 'em all the way back to Utah. But we'll leave that for now. Them two killers are locked up, so I can rest easy. Had a helluva time bringin' 'em in. Wouldn't't've bothered you 'cept it was pretty close to here when I caught up with 'em.'

'You crossed another state line to bring 'em here, Barney.'

'Well — hell, I wanted to see how you're gettin' on, kid — and I had me a hankerin' to taste Lucille's fine cookin'.' He winked at the woman, obviously trying to get her on side, but she affected not to hear, moved out to the kitchen with the dirty dishes.

'Well, kinfolk are always welcome, Barney.'

'Good to know.' There was a twist to Barney's mouth when he said that but he covered it quickly by running his tongue along the edge of the cigarette paper, completing his smoke. Monte remained silent while his brother lit up and exhaled some smoke. 'You know folk around here pretty well by now, I guess, huh, kid?'

'I ain't been a 'kid' for a helluva long time, Barney. But yeah, I know a lot of folk. Have to be tough with 'em sometimes, hence the gallows we built to sort of remind 'em I don't play favourites. But they know they're payin' me to keep the law as best I can and that's what I do — the best I can.'

'Yeah, well, I guess I taught you good.' Barney was taking credit where it wasn't due and if he saw Monte's crooked smile at his words, he chose to ignore it. 'Lookin' for an Injun family, Sioux, I think. Two bucks and a squaw. She's a real looker for a redskin, used to be with a tourin' company, doin' an act on stage with the bucks . . . '

Monte frowned and glanced towards the kitchen.

'Now you keep your voice down if you're workin' up to some dirty talk!'

Barney chuckled. 'No, no! I din' mean that kinda act. It don't matter about the damn act anyway! Thing is, they stole some gold from some whites and the word is they come back to this neck of the woods and bought a big ranch near here.'

'No Injuns runnin' a ranch anywhere

around here, I can tell you that for sure! Hell, folk just wouldn't stand for it. They'd lynch 'em, and I think I'd turn a blind eye to it.'

'That's what I figured. Maybe in the next county?'

'Not between here and Montana — nor Nebraska and the Dakotas. Judas, somethin' like that'd be talked about all over the Territory! Injuns buyin' a *ranch*!'

Barney dragged on his cigarette, frowning now.

'You sure? I mean, could they've put up the money and had some white man front for 'em? Put the ranch in his name but they're the real owners?'

Monte scratched his head.

'Well, I dunno. I've never come across anythin' like that. Why would they do it? You know Injuns: if they've got money they spend it, and if it's a lot of money, they spend up big. They don't like the kinda work white men do.'

Barney swore under his breath. This

was a set-back. He'd felt certain sure that his brother, if anyone, would know about such a thing. In more ways than one, Monte Wales was turning out to be a big disappointment to his elder brother.

Maybe he better have a word with that Geary, in his cell with the door locked. He was the one told Nolan about the ranch up here and Barney was sure it wasn't a lie just for *his* benefit. At that time neither prisoner had suspected that the passage was acting as a mighty fine sound channel for conversations between prisoners in their cells.

He was about to try and skim over it now when Monte spoke again.

'Just thinkin'. There was a new tradin' post or Indian Agency opened up on the Elk Mountain reservation, west of Laramie. Mebbe a year back now. Dunno much about it but I heard it's run by the Injuns themselves. Some sort of experimental deal with the Territorial Council — tryin' to clean up after all them scandals with government-appointed agents robbin' the redskins blind. The do-gooders and bleedin'-hearts stepped in on the Injuns' behalf. Believe a young squaw and her father were the ones set it up. Dunno who else was involved. Or even if they're still around.'

Barney was leaning forward in his chair now, eyes bright.

'That sounds like it has possibilities. They might've dropped the young buck off somewheres along the way. To hell with him, anyway. What's the nearest town? Laramie?'

Monte shook his head. 'It's not too far away but Longbow's closer.'

'You know the sheriff there?'

'It ain't got a sheriff. The Laramie lawman looks after it. It's still in his county, though the reservation is on its own piece of gov'ment land. Got its own police.'

'How about you take me across to Laramie tomorrow and make the introductions? Then we'll go on to this Longbow.'

Monte frowned. 'It's a far piece, Barney! Not just round the next bend! This is Big Sky country up here, man!'

'C'mon, Monte! We're brothers! Anythin' I turn up I'll cut you in on, you know that.'

'Like you used to when we was growin' up? As I recollect I was the one always got the fat lip and the small share of anythin', from candy on up!'

Barney laughed. 'You got a damn long memory, Monte, ol' son. But you're forgettin' a coupla things, ain't you? Like, who was it took care of you after Ma and Pa died, huh? I had to be kinda hard on you for your own good. Hell, Pa was the same with all of us kids, you know that.'

'Aaaah.' Monte sounded and looked part-embarrassed and part angry. 'All right. I'll take you over tomorrow. But I don't want to leave Lucille alone for long in this town.'

Barney winked. 'Don't blame you. I'd say Lucille ain't only good at cookin' . . . ' He saw his brother's face changing and hurried on. 'I mean, she's right fine company and a good-looker. I savvy how you wouldn't want to leave her alone. No, that's fine, ki — Monte. You just get me to Laramie or Longbow and I'll take it from there.'

Monte nodded and began to make his own cigarette, wondering just what big brother Barney was up to.

It had taken him a long, long time to realize he didn't have to do exactly as Barney told him, big brother or not. He had a mind of his own and Ma had taught *him* right from wrong, even if Pa had looked at things different — and spent a deal of time in jail because of such thinking.

Since marrying Lucille he liked to think he had matured and was now independent of Barney. Hadn't seen the man in years — hadn't even known he'd left the army and taken up a sheriff's job — and wasn't all that pleased at seeing him now. But, kin or not, Barney Wales better not try to pull some smart law-bending shuffle while he was in *his* county.

He smiled thinly. Be a pleasure to teach him something about 'jurisdiction' after all the beatings Barney had dealt him over the years, on that subject and a hundred others.

OK! He admitted he was a little afraid of his brother, knowing how violent and ruthless the man could be, but if it came time to really assert himself, then he would do the best he could. Like always . . .

Yeah, whatever Barney was up to had better be legit or there was going to be a family falling-out. A *big* one.

★   ★   ★

Barney Wales turned in early, weary after the long days on the trail north, and eager to be fresh for the ride to Laramie in the morning.

Monte lay in the big rumpled double bed beside the sleeping Lucille, awake, hands clasped behind his head. Then abruptly he eased out of bed, pulled on trousers and left the room.

When he reached the cell block, he had a lantern in one hand, a sixgun in the other. He ran the barrel along the barred windows in the cell doors, waking both Nolan and Geary. They blinked at him and he stood back between the doors so he could talk to both at the same time.

'Brother Barney tells me you two murdered five men in cold blood.'

'That's his story,' Nolan said after a pause.

'What's yours?'

Nolan strained to see what he could of Geary.

'Reckon it's worth losing sleep to tell our side, Bob?'

'Can't hurt. You heard of a man runs a tradin' post in Utah called Tad Marney, Sheriff . . . ?'

'Reckon there wouldn't be a lawman in the country hasn't heard of Tad at one time or another.'

'OK. Well, it's his bunch we're s'posed to've murdered.'

'We killed two when they tried to bushwhack us,' Nolan added, 'wounded two, and one got away. Alive!'

They told the story succinctly and Monte listened without interruption. He looked from one man to the other when they had finished.

'Sounds like it coulda happened that way. But Barney says he found all five dead, at least one man backshot, which sounds more like murder than self-defence.'

'He's either lyin' or someone else did it after we hightailed it,' Nolan said carefully, noting the way the sheriff's eyes narrowed when he called Barney a liar.

'Tell me about the gold — and these Injuns.'

Nolan strained again to see Geary's face, caught a glimpse, saw the man's thinned-out lips.

'Brother Barney's following through on what he heard when he eavesdropped on our cell, Bob.'

Monte was frowning now, had pushed off the wall and stood straight.

'What's this?'

'Didn't you know Barney has a special passage from his law office to the cell block that carries sound right to him? Claims he learns a helluva lot from prisoners thinking it's safe to talk in their cells . . . '

Monte blew out his cheeks slowly. Barney had always been sneaky and devious — this sounded like him, all right.

'All right. Just what did he overhear that's got him all goosed-up?'

Nolan sensed that while Monte might be Barney's young brother, he was from a different mould. He took a chance and settled down to tell the man everything.

*   *   *

It was a mighty hot day and Barney had almost emptied his canteen as they came down from a ridge, allowing the mounts to pick their own trail. Capping the vessel, he looked sidelong at his brother.

'You ain't hardly had a word to say in all the miles we've travelled, l'il brother.' Monte looked up and shrugged. Barney grinned lecherously. 'Lucille keepin' you too busy, is she?'

He tensed when Monte stiffened, gave him a bleak look.

'Watch your tongue!'

'Hell, I only meant with work around the place — like them new cupboards she's got you buildin' in the kitchen and the new wash-bench. What you think I meant?' He put on his innocent face and Monte scowled.

'I know what you meant. I'm not a mornin' person, Barney. Be all right after we stop for coffee and some vittals.'

Barney Wales grunted, but he wondered . . . He thought he'd heard someone moving around last night and, listening in his bed, there had been a dull thud that he knew only the heavy door

136

between the law office and the cell-block made when closing . . .

Monte had surprised him in his tough manner this time. He had sure done some growing-up in the years since they had last seen each other. Might have to watch his step . . .

The sheriff of Laramie was a little cock-sparrow of a man with a reputation that would have suited someone twice his size. His name was Dakota Case and he sported a heavy frontier moustache and mutton-chop sideburns. His hair was slicked tight to his skull, his eyes bleak as he shook hands perfunctorily with Barney.

'Heard of you. Never made the connection with Monte.' The cold eyes flicked from one man to the other. 'Never take you for brothers.'

'We went our separate ways a long time ago,' Barney said with a grin that had no effect whatsoever on the sober Case.

'Yeah, well, Monte's a damn good man and lawman and he has my respect.'

Barney wasn't comfortable at the way Case looked at him. The small man didn't beat about the bush, either.

'You here to make trouble for these people in the Agency at Elk Mountain?'

'Hell, no! I mean . . . I'm mostly here to check out the story that they stole some gold from the two prisoners I brought in and got stowed in Monte's hoosegow right now.' He widened the grin. 'Like to give a man every chance to prove his innocence before I see him strung up.'

'They gotta be tried yet, Barney,' Monte reminded him curtly.

Barney frowned. 'What you know about it — apart from what I told you, l'il brother?'

'Had a talk with Nolan and Geary after you went to bed. They got a different version of things.'

Barney Wales's smile stiffened at the edges. 'Oh . . . ?'

'Their story sounds possible. Like you say, they oughta be given every chance to prove their side of things before *anyone* thinks of puttin' a rope round their necks.'

'Uh-huh. So that's why you were so damn tired this mornin'. Kinda sneaky, kid.'

Monte shrugged and held his brother's gaze. Barney obviously didn't like it a hell of a lot. Dakota Case flicked his hard eyes to big Barney.

'Someone better gimme all the facts — and I mean *all*. I ain't no Injun-lover but I got a mandate from Department of Indian Affairs to keep an eye on that agency at Elk Mountain . . . And if you didn't know already, I'm a man who takes his work seriously.'

Both Wales's knew that. Barney showed his displeasure in the way he glared at Monte and snapped at him during the telling of the story behind Nolan's and Geary's arrest. Barney's version was embellished, of course, to put him in the best light possible, but Case's chiselled features gave nothing away.

When they had finished, the little

sheriff stood up.

'Monte, you stayin' or goin' back?'

'Reckon I'll head back, Dakota. Don't like leavin' Lucille. My deputy's off with chicken-pox, of all things.'

Case reached for his hat and gun belt on a peg.

'All right, Barney. Let's you and me hit the trail. We'll spend the night at Longbow, go up the mountain in the mornin' and see what this squaw's got to say for herself.'

Barney nodded, but didn't look too happy.

8

A Kind of Freedom

Nolan smiled through the barred window in his cell door as he pushed his empty dishes through the trap lower down where Lucille Wales collected them.

'That was an elegant meal, Mrs Wales. Years since I've tasted roast pork, seasoned just right and with crunchy cracklin'.'

Lucille looked pleased, flushed a little, even more when Geary added his praise from his own cell.

'Well, Monte likes his prisoners to eat well. He always says you never know if it's going to be their last meal or — Oh! I'm sorry! I . . . I didn't mean to sound so . . . pessimistic.'

Nolan smiled thinly. 'That's all right, ma'am. If we can help it, we ain't gonna christen that there new gallows that throws its shadow right across the cell block come sundown.'

'Yes — er — Monte doesn't like that . . . symbolism, either. He doesn't really want to, but he told me he tends to believe your version of . . . things.' She added quickly: 'Not that he's calling his brother a liar, but he does think Barney could have gotten things . . . wrong, in his enthusiasm to keep his record as a good lawman . . . intact.'

'That's good to know, Mrs Wales, because neither Bob nor me are killers. We'll protect ourselves, sure, but we don't go hunting trouble. I give you my word on that.'

Lucille was becoming uncomfortable now and he guessed she didn't want to be seen as either siding with her husband or going against Barney. Although it was obvious she did not hold a very high opinion of the elder Wales brother.

'I'll bring you some coffee later,' she said and started to move away carrying the dirty dishes.

'Look forward to it, ma'am,' Nolan called and gestured quickly to Geary who added,

'Me, too. Good food and good company is somethin' we don't get a lot of on the drift.'

She broke her step briefly but didn't look around, kept going to the passage door.

'You going to work on her?' Geary asked when she had gone.

'You're the ladies' man.'

'Yeah, and she's a looker but . . .' He shook his head slowly. 'She wouldn't do anything to go agin her husband.'

'Mebbe not, but she's a good-hearted woman. Wouldn't want one of the prisoners she's responsible for to fall sick — specially if she thought it was caused by her cooking . . .'

Slowly, Geary smiled. 'They sure taught you some sneaky things in Yuma!'

★ ★ ★

It worked.

When Lucille brought the coffee she paused after opening the passage door. She thought she had heard a moan . . . She had! Coming from Mr Nolan's cell . . . She hurried down the passage.

'Is . . . everything all right?'

Geary appeared at his barred window, gripping tightly, his knuckles white.

'Oh, ma'am! I been yellin' myself hoarse. It's my pard! He's been throwin' up, has these griping stomach pains. Says he . . . I'm sorry, Mrs Wales, but he thinks it was something in your pork. Seasonin', mebbe.'

'Oh!' She put a hand to her mouth almost dropping the small tray of coffee and biscuits, hurriedly set it down. 'I — I'll have to get the keys I suppose. Or perhaps I should send for the doctor first — '

'Ma'am, I'd be obliged if you'd take a look at him right away,' Geary said quickly. 'He's been throwin' up somethin' awful and — well, he managed to tell me the bucket's full an' near overflowing . . . '

'Oh, my goodness! What have I done!' She was almost in tears as she hurried back to the front office and came back carrying the ring of keys. As she fumbled to find the right one, Geary kept up a patter about how he was sure it must be something other than her fine cooking, that Nolan had seen a sawbones once before for a similar attack and the doctor had thought it might be appendicitis.

'Goodness! I hope not. Ah, this is the right one.'

She unlocked the door and hurried across the cell to where Nolan writhed on the bunk, knees drawn up to his chest, face contorted, moaning convincingly.

'Let me see, Mr Nolan. I — I'll have to loosen your belt but . . . ' As she spoke she glanced in the corner at the slop-bucket, saw that it was empty. Her head snapped around. 'I — I don't understand . . . Oh!'

By then Nolan was off the bunk. He grabbed her arm gently but firmly, easing the ring of keys out of her hand.

He spoke quietly.

'I'm sorry, Mrs Wales. There was nothing wrong with your pork. It's likely the best meal I've ever had, but — well, we can't stay here. That brother-in-law of yours is keen to put a rope around our necks.'

She recovered quite quickly, gave him a slow smile.

'You young devil! *Both* of you! Making my head spin with compliments when all the time . . . Oh, I don't think you're going to harm me so don't look so worried. I'm not going to faint or scream hysterically. I'll just have a rest on the bunk after you lock me in. Though you could slide in the tray of coffee and biscuits first . . . '

Nolan blinked: he hadn't expected this kind of reaction. Then he smiled, turned and smoothed out the rumpled blanket on the narrow bunk.

'You're a real lady, Mrs Wales.'

'Oh, far from it! Nice of you to say so, though.' She widened her smile. 'I never did take to Barney. A big bully. It was good this time to see Monte stand up to him and — well, if Monte doubts his story, that's fine with me. I wish you luck, gentlemen, but I must warn you: Barney Wales can be one of the meanest, and most persistent men who ever walked this earth when he's crossed.'

'I sure hope it don't backfire on you,' Geary said as Nolan released him. He picked up the coffee tray and carried it into Nolan's cell, setting it down for Mrs Wales who was now sitting on the edge of the bunk.

On impulse, he leaned down and kissed her cheek. She looked at him sharply but smiled as she rubbed the place gently.

'My, my. I think you two had better be on your way!'

They wasted no more time.

★　★　★

It was very late when Monte Wales returned and his frantic calls to her woke Lucille in the cell. She was about to reply but decided to wait and in a few minutes her wild-eyed husband came hurrying down the passage carrying a lantern.

'Lucille? You in here . . . ?'

'Is that you, Monte . . . ?'

'Oh, Jesus!' he said with vast relief, running the rest of the way. 'I been lookin' everywhere for you!'

When he saw her standing at the bars of the cell door window, smiling at him, he blinked. 'What . . . ?'

'It's rather a long story, dear. Can you get me out of here and we'll go back to the house and I'll cook you some supper and tell you all about it.'

'Hell, never mind the supper. I'll have to get after them prisoners! How in the hell did they . . . ?'

He held her close and she clung to him. 'I'll tell you over supper,' she whispered in his ear. 'You look tired, dear. You've had a very long ride. I think you should get a good night's sleep before you worry about those two gentlemen.'

He stepped back.

'Gentlemen . . . ? They been sweet-talkin' you?'

'Oh, ye-es, I suppose they were, but they were very nice, very gentle, didn't harm me in any way, made me comfortable — '

'Judas, Lucille! These are *murderers*!'

'Oh, I don't believe that — and neither do you, deep down. It's that brother of yours. He's after their gold and nothing else. Except to make sure they hang so they can't make trouble for him. Now you know I'm right, Monte . . . '

He sighed, half-nodded.

'But I took an oath of office, Lucille, to uphold the law — and they were prisoners in my custody. If they've escaped, I have to go after them.'

'Well, we'll talk about it over a hot meal . . . '

'*Lucille!*'

'Come along, Monte — I'm starving.'

He threw up his hands and followed her down the passage.

'Believin' their story and lettin' 'em get away are two different things, Lucille.'

'Of course, you're right, dear. But it makes sense to have a substantial meal and a good night's rest before setting out after fugitives, surely . . . ?'

He saw he couldn't win.

Anyway, it would be something to look forward to — seeing the look on Barney's face when he told him the prisoners had escaped.

★ ★ ★

'We're bound to run into Barney,' Geary said as they rode through the night. 'If he's not still in Laramie, he'll be in Longbow or up at the agency.'

Nolan had been thinking the same thing but he waited before answering until they had worked their horses down a steep slope that led them into a narrow ravine with a high, thin waterfall on their left. They filled their water-bottles and there was enough starlight

150

for them to load their guns. They had found the weapons in Monte's office but they had been unloaded. Nolan had grabbed a cardboard box of cartridges on the way out but now found it was only half-full.

'Not gonna have many bullets to spare,' he opined as they thumbed home the loads. 'The Laramie sheriff could be waiting for us if Monte gets off a telegraph message right away.'

'Aw, I reckon the lovely Lucille will keep him kind of interested until daylight.'

'You got a helluva lot of faith in your sugar-talk!'

Geary winked. 'Had lots of practice. I can pick a passionate woman when I see one.'

'Well, sorry, pard, but I don't aim to count on that happening.'

Geary frowned. 'What you got in mind?'

'Let's get outta this ravine and I'll show you.'

It took them almost two hours to find

their way out and up on to the short-grass prairie. By that time, the moon had risen and silver light washed like water over the prairie, clearly showing the distant line of telegraph poles.

Nolan spurred ahead and Geary, startled, was several seconds late in urging his own mount on. By that time, Nolan was sitting astride his now stationary horse, rifle to his shoulder. Geary jumped as the rifle crashed, the shot exploding through the night, going away in a series of diminishing drum-rolls across the night. To his left he saw a shower of sparks, heard something like glass shattering. He settled his skittish mount and put it alongside Nolan as the man fired again with the same result — sparks and shattering glass, coming from the dim, gallows-like poles.

'Why didn't I think of that?' Geary said, grinning, as Nolan fired a third time. 'Three insulators gone for ever and the telegraph wire down in three places. Hell, it'll be days before they get it repaired.'

'*If* they got spare insulators,' Nolan said. 'It ought to give us time to catch up with Barney.'

'He won't be expectin' us, that's for sure.' Geary stood in the stirrups, looked around a little anxiously. 'Hope that shooting don't stir up any Injuns wanderin' this here prairie.'

'If it does, we'd better make a run for it. Can't afford any more ammo.' Nolan started to turn his horse. 'Reckon we'll need every last bullet when Barney Wales finds out we've busted loose.'

They rode on into the night, apprehensive, but the only alarm was when they disturbed a small herd of bison in a hollow and the animals leapt up as one and thundered off into the darkness.

It was barely daylight when they sighted Longbow, having skirted around Laramie hours earlier.

It was a small town at the foot of Elk Mountain and already a few chimneys showed smoke from the early-morning cooking-fires in the shacks and cabins.

Lucille Wales's pork meal had long since been digested and they were both hungry. Nolan stole a half-dozen eggs from a chicken-coop, disturbing the birds, but making it out of the yard before the owner reached for his shotgun.

They stopped by a creek at the foot of the mountain trail and cooked the eggs on a small, hidden fire, washed them down with water. By then the sun was spreading light all across the countryside and they saw two riders leaving Longbow, heading in their direction.

'One of 'em's Barney Wales,' Geary said, focusing his battered old army field glasses. 'Other one's — hell! Thought it was a kid he's so small, but he's got a moustache and . . . Ah, must be the Laramie sheriff, Dakota Case. Judas, Matt, I'd rather it was only Wales we had to go up against! Case is hell on wheels! Hard as granite and quick on the draw.'

'OK — then we've got to dodge him. I lived up here a long time back, and I think I can find a way up to that agency that doesn't follow the regular trail.'

Geary was still uncertain, watching the two riders.

'They'll be makin' for there, too! We're gonna run into 'em sooner or later.'

'Then we'll make it later. C'mon. Let's move.'

⋆　⋆　⋆

It was not an easy trail.

Not only was it steep and winding, but some of the bends were hairpin, doubled back on themselves. The edges of the trail were crumbling and once Geary's mount's hindfeet broke away the dirt and stones. It whickered in fear, hunched and lunged with a violence that almost unseated its rider.

Nolan had his rope already shaken out and although he saw now that it wasn't really necessary, he tossed a loop to his pard. Geary grabbed it gratefully.

'I've never been a man for heights!' he said, wiping sweat from his face as the horse settled on to firmer ground.

'Make sure you ride close in against the wall,' advised Nolan, hanging his lariat over the saddle horn again.

Geary nodded, looked back and down. 'No sign of them lawmen.'

'Shouldn't be — we're climbing the opposite side of the mountain to them.'

'They gonna get there before us?'

'Shouldn't wonder.'

'Hope there's cover overlooking the agency then.'

'Lot of brush and some timber as I recall. But just remember we're on a reservation now. Could run into some Sioux.'

'Why do I always pick pardners who look on the bright side of things!'

Nolan grinned. 'Practice, I reckon.'

They lost a lot of sweat and the horses were blowing by the time they reached the top. As Nolan had recollected, there was brush and scattered timber. From where they came out they could see across open ground, over a winding creek, to the Indian encampment.

Tipis were scattered all along the creek and some backed into the rising slopes behind. There were maybe forty or fifty altogether and the two men could make out the colours of the paintings on the buckskin sides from here, though not the detail. Indians moved about, some women and children, some men. They all seemed to have a job to interest them.

Young boys watched over the herd of pintos, amusing themselves by wrestling and practising fighting with sticks. Men were sitting around in groups, playing their dice-games, smoking, and Nolan recognized at least one sweat lodge, steam and smoke coming through the layers of bark.

It was a peaceful scene, women tending corn and other crops, some suckling babies, others making buckskin clothes, chewing the hide to soften it for their menfolk, scraping fat or pegging hides on drying-frames. Others made pemmican balls.

Beyond were the log buildings of the agency, the corrals holding horses and a few beef cattle, sheds for storing the grain and agency goods.

'By hell, this must be the Happy Hunting Grounds far as those bucks are concerned,' opined Geary.

'Looks like an old-time encampment,' allowed Nolan slowly. 'Like Custer used to love to attack — hit 'em while they were quiet and minding their own business. Guess this is what a reservation was meant to look like, but not many do.'

Geary hitched around from where they lay stretched out under some brush.

'You reckon any of our gold went into making this place?'

Nolan's glance was sharp. His forehead creased slightly.

'We-ell. Just might be,' he said thoughtfully. 'Old Black Wolf hated the whites and seems he taught Abby to do the same. Never thought about the gold being put to this kind of use, though.'

'*If* it has. It was just a thought.'

'Hmmm. Oh-oh! Here comes the law!'

They tensed as they saw Barney Wales and Dakota Case ride in and stop outside the biggest building of the agency. There was movement as the door opened and Geary heard Nolan's breath suck in sharply as he recognized Abby, or 'Fawn Lightfoot' as she was called by the tribe. He reached out and touched Nolan's arm.

'Easy, pard.'

Nolan grunted, his eyes narrowed as he watched the lawmen dismount and face Abby. After a few words were exchanged she went back into the building. Wales and Case followed. Nolan and Geary tensed as a door in a large barn-like building opened a little way and they glimpsed a man in the shadows. He looked like an Indian in buckskin, holding a lever-action rifle.

He was watching the door of the long building intently.

'Now, what's he doing?' Nolan muttered.

'At a guess, I'd say standin' guard,' said Geary, then added quietly: 'Thought Injuns weren't allowed repeating rifles.'

'They're not. Just single-shot for hunting on the reservations. We better stay put, see what happens.'

'That's good advice, feller,' said a cold voice from behind them. 'You twitch an eyelid and I'll blow your goddamn head off!'

9

Elk Mountain

The inside of the Agency was dim, though reflected light through the window-spaces with the shutters propped open was adequate. The lawmen looked around, Dakota Case with one small hand on the rounded butt of his Smith & Wesson pistol. Barney Wales had thought on the way up that the standard butt of a Colt would have been too large for the small sheriff. The S&W type seemed just about right.

Abby, wearing a long buckskin dress, her hair braided, dark eyes glittering, went behind the counter and faced the men. Shelves of various cans and packages rose behind her.

'Wolf is not here. He is working with some of our braves, teaching them about what you whites call 'animal husbandry'.'

'That so?' Barney Wales said, his eyes undressing the beautiful woman.

'And how would he know about a *white* man thing like that?' said Case.

Abby met the small lawman's gaze steadily.

'He knows.' There was pride and certainty in those two short words. 'Indians have lived with Nature longer than whites!' There was contempt in those words.

'Wolf knows lots of things, does he?' persisted Case.

'Wolf is wise. Can I help you?'

Case glanced at Wales, clearly giving him the floor. Barney thumbed back his hat, licking his lips as he stared at Abby, his thoughts obvious.

'Get yourself off heat,' the small sheriff snapped. 'You want to start another Indian war?'

'Wouldn't mind — if she was one of the prizes!' Wales laughed as he said the words, saw the flash of fire in her eyes. 'Relax, darlin'. We're here on official business.'

'What is it?' Abby's voice sounded edgy with suppressed anger.

'Whoo-eeee! You sure don't like us white-eyes, do you?'

Impatiently, Case said: 'Ma'am, Wales here has two prisoners back in Cheyenne and they claim you stole some gold from them.'

Abby was clearly surprised and her thin dark eyebrows arched. There was a small pause before she replied.

'Gold? We run a reservation here, Sheriff Case, and all our money comes from the Department of Indian Affairs in Washington — plus a few dollars from sympathetic people from time to time.'

'Sympathetic *white* people, I guess you mean.'

Her gaze did not waver. 'A . . . few. Some of our own people work for the whites, save their money, give it to help the tribe.'

Case smiled crookedly. 'And you like that little bit of independence, don't you.'

Abby's small, rounded jaw tilted at him.

'Of course. That is the aim of this . . . experiment. What is the word your politicians use? 'Self-sufficiency'?'

'I guess that'll do . . . '

'Feller called Matt Nolan claims he married you and you stole gold belongin' to him and his pard, Bob Geary — a lot of gold.'

Her face was suddenly blank.

'I am an unmarried Indian woman, Sheriff.'

Wales snorted and Case narrowed his eyes. 'I've heard it said before that you Injuns regard any of your people who marry a white as 'unmarried' because they won't recognize the white man's way of life, or his laws or his faith: they want to stick to their own ways.'

She smiled, surprising them.

'You have knowledge of our people, I see, Sheriff. No, we don't like the white man's ways.'

'You earned a livin' from 'em in Arizona!' Wales snapped. 'You and your old man and your brother — '

'Half-brother,' she corrected him, unsmiling now. 'Yes — it was . . . convenient. Wolf is wise enough to see that our only chance of survival is to co-operate with the whites when it suits us, so we can become 'self-sufficient'.' She made it sound like a curse. 'It suits us to use your ways at times, for our own ends and because we know we *must* . . . adapt.'

'Or go under,' Case said succinctly, hard-eyed. Wales was frowning now.

'I seen your act once or twice. You din' speak American so well then.'

She smiled again. 'I just didn't speak it very much at all, Sheriff. You learn a lot more when people think you don't understand their language. Your General Custer was a believer in such a thing — pretended not to understand our language, then used what information he gathered against us!'

She couldn't hide the burning hatred sounding in her voice or showing in her eyes. The very name of Custer made her slim body tremble. Wales frowned deeper but Case seemed suddenly more alert.

'We're getting off the subject. Nolan and Geary and their gold, ma'am, is what we want to know about.'

Abby drew down a deep breath.

'I know Mr Nolan and Mr Geary. They seemed . . . interesting for whites. They mentioned they had found a lot of gold in Sonora but I — we — my father and brother as well — never saw any of it.' She smiled faintly. 'I think it was just talk, their way of trying to impress me. I was . . . popular with a lot of whites. Many tried to impress me with wild claims, obviously false. If you saw our stage tableau, Sheriff Wales, you will understand . . . '

'You can say that again! Man, the amount of sweat that audience oozed each time you came on stage — '

'Then you deny the charges that you stole any gold?' cut in Case, determined to keep things on track.

'Of course I do!' she snapped. 'I have

166

no husband, white or Indian! I know nothing about any stolen gold. Now, would you like to see around our reservation? See just how we put our meagre funds to use? We are trying to keep to our old way of life while at the same time adapting certain ways of the white man that we believe can benefit us . . . '

'We ain't no Washington committee you have to impress, lady,' Wales growled. 'But from what I seen ridin' in you can't be too short of funds! Mebbe we should take a look at your books!'

Abby's smile was wide, ready to oblige and co-operate.

'You have the papers from Washington? The proper authority, signed and authorized by the administrator?'

Wales scowled and Case touched his arm.

'C'mon, Wales. We're wastin' time here. The Injuns have got us out-smarted — for the moment.'

'Thank you, Sheriff Case!' Abby said, still smiling. 'At last, a small Indian victory! Not known since the days of Red Cloud and the Bozeman Trail. *And the Little Big Horn!*'

Wales seemed disinclined to move.

'She's laughin at us! I don't like no Injun, good-lookin' squaw or not, laughin' at *me*!'

'Wales! This is Federal land. We have no jurisdiction here. I have to live in this neck of the woods and while you might think you can kick up your heels, bust a few heads, you ain't gonna do it while I have a say in it!'

It was clear Abby was enjoying the sudden conflict between the white men and Wales was smart enough to realize it. He snarled *Aaaagh*! spat on the floor and stormed out.

Case touched his hatbrim to the now sober woman.

'We *might* be back, ma'am. These men in Cheyenne could swing on their brand-new gallows if you don't back their story about the gold — and your alleged rape that set Nolan on the trail of two he killed on your behalf.'

She stared coolly. 'I don't know what you're talking about, Sheriff. Goodbye.'

The lawmen mounted in silence, looked around the peaceful scene, especially at the encampment down along the creek with work-busy Indians.

'I wish Custer was waitin' in the wings right now!' growled Wales as he turned his horse. 'I'd give him the high-sign and lead him in with all guns blazin'!'

'There's been enough of that, Wales,' Case said without heat but in a tone that ended any speculation. 'Thought I saw some mounted men going through that timber across the creek while we were talkin' to her. White men by the saddles and guns.'

Wales scowled but stared, trying to make it casual.

'Don't see nothin'. But I dunno as I'm goin' back to Longbow, Case.'

Dakota snapped his head up.

'Why? I told you, this is Federal land. We've no right here.'

'I don't care if it's inside the Pearly

Gates. There's somethin' goin' on here. I never expected that squaw to admit to anythin' but she sure hates our guts and didn't try to hide it. She's too damn confident, too . . . touchy.'

'You didn't try to hide what you wanted to do, either! Judas, Wales, I didn't think you could be that stupid.'

'You go to hell, Case! I don't need you!'

'The reservation's Federal land, the rest is in my jurisdiction. You just think along those lines for a bit. Meantime, you come on back to Longbow with me.'

Wales reined in, his big, coarse face hard.

'Who the hell you orderin' around?'

Case sat his horse casually, small hands folded on his saddle horn. He saw Wales's tensed shoulders, the right arm crooked, ready to flex into a fast draw.

'You.'

'Well, mebbe I'll just have somethin' to say about that!'

'Why not? You talk plenty.'

That did it. Barney Wales reached for his gun, froze with his hand not quite touching the butt. He stared unbelievingly down the barrel of Dakota Case's Smith & Wesson, held rock-steady in a small fist.

'Just come along, Barney,' Case said steadily. 'I don't want to shoot you — 'less I have to. Then I will. You can believe that.'

Wales did, swallowed, let his hand drop, clearing his dry throat as he let his shoulders settle and relax.

'We don't have to get into a spat.'

'Glad you see it that way.' But Case did not holster his pistol right away. 'You sure ain't like your brother.'

'Maybe that makes me lucky! Monte's lost his ambition; he ain't goin' nowhere.'

'I dunno. Sheriff of a town like Cheyenne must mean somethin'. How big's that place where you put up your feet, Barney?'

'Go to hell!' Barney growled again.

But he was shaking with barely suppressed anger.

As the lawmen disappeared down the mountain trail, Abby closed the door and leaned against it. Black Wolf came out of the small storeroom at the other end of the building, holding a shiny new Winchester rifle.

'The one called Wales will be back,' he said. 'He is the greedy one. He knows that gold came here. Telling him it is all spent will do nothing to discourage him.'

'We should post more look-outs.' They were conversing in the Sioux language.

'That will be done. But I think there are others already here.' Wolf gestured through the open window towards the creek, where there was a good deal of movement now, men hurrying into the woods, the women ceasing their soil-tilling and other chores. They had played their peaceful role — for now. Abby frowned at Wolf's words.

'Who is it?'

'I will see. There was someone down at the boulders at the edge of the trees. Where McAlpine and Bodie were. I only glimpsed it while the lawmen were here. I think they captured two whites spying on the camp . . . '

He made for the door. She was looking very sober now.

'It could not be . . . Matthew?' She asked.

Wolf shook his head, his gaze unnerving her.

'Will I come?'

Wolf shook his head again, suddenly handed her the rifle.

'It is best if we do not yet carry weapons openly.'

She ran her hands caressingly over the cold blue steel of the gun's sleek lines as he went out.

'Some day soon you will speak for the Sioux,' she murmured.

★ ★ ★

They both knew their captors: Bodie and McAlpine, a couple of army

173

deserters who had turned up on the Sonora goldfields and quickly established a reputation as claim-jumpers and murderers. In the end, their exploits became too constant and unacceptable and they fled the fields just ahead of a lynch mob.

Both Nolan and Geary had seen them again in Tucson and other towns in Arizona, where they had raised hell in celebratory wingdings. Once they had found them going through their things in a rented room and, getting the jump, had beaten them badly before flinging both down the outside stairway of the saloon. They sustained some bad injuries, Bodie a broken collar-bone and ribs, McAlpine a busted arm and ribs, concussion and badly wrenched ankle. They had been inconvenienced for a long, long time, during which their raging hatred for Nolan and Bob Geary had plenty of opportunity to grow and nurture.

This was their first meeting since those days and it was mighty clear from the outset that neither man had forgotten their last meeting.

It was Bodie who had found them watching the agency and the lawmen. McAlpine was close by and came running at Bodie's low whistle.

'You been rubbin' that ol' rabbitfoot of yours, Mac?' Bodie asked, keeping his rifle trained on the prostrate men at his feet. 'Looky at the surprise I got for you!'

'Well, damn if all my birthdays ain't come at once!' McAlpine, tall, gangly, beard-shagged, but wearing fairly good clothes, stepped forward, stomped on the backs of both Geary and Nolan, grinding in his high heels.

'C'mon, Bode, let's git these two where we can have us some real fun!' McAlpine kicked the men again and kept kicking until, staggering, gasping for breath, grunting in pain, Nolan and Geary crawled back into the thicker brush at Bodie's command, then eased up to their feet, swaying. McAlpine was all set to start in busting teeth but

Bodie, almost as tall but broader and harder-looking, stopped him.

'Just a minute, Mac. Old Wolf'll want to see these two. I happen to know he has somethin' special planned for 'em. He figured they'd show up sometime.'

But Wolf was mighty surprised to see the ex-miners when he arrived on the scene.

'Sheriff Case has just told us you were in the Cheyenne jail, waiting to hang,' the old Indian said flatly.

'Couldn't keep away when we heard you were here, you old bastard,' growled Geary.

It was excuse enough for McAlpine to ram his rifle butt against the man's spine, dropping him, gasping, to his knees. Wolf showed no emotion, flicked his gaze to the silent Nolan.

'You found a way to escape, No-lan.' Nolan didn't bother to reply. 'I would like to see you swinging at the end of a rope, No-lan, but perhaps it is better that you are here.'

Nolan frowned. 'Why? Because I married Abby?'

Wolf scoffed. 'No! It meant nothing to her — it was just a way to get our hands on your gold more easily.'

Nolan seemed puzzled. 'How about that rape? She really had been beaten . . . '

Wolf's face hardened. He took a while to answer.

'Horse Catcher.'

Both Nolan and Geary blinked. McAlpine and Bodie waited impatiently, but they seemed deferential to Wolf.

'What d'you mean — Horse Catcher? You saying he raped her? His own sister?' Nolan was bewildered.

'Half-sister. Yes! He was always very . . . caring . . . about her. You whites might call it 'love' but we have no word for it in our language. I think your word might be . . . obsessed.'

'Jesus, that's sick!' Geary opined vehemently.

'Yes!' Wolf agreed heavily. 'Horse Catcher was 'sick' about Fawn. Strictly forbidden by the tribe, brother and sister! The penalty is . . . severe.'

He said no more and Nolan asked gently:

'You followed him to the camp, was too late to save Abby, then went after Horse — and caught him up?'

Wolf merely stared coldly.

'Judas priest!' breathed Geary, staring hard at Wolf. 'It was you did those god-awful things to him!'

Wolf's jaw was square and iron-hard.

'It is the law of the tribe. The punishment is clear!'

'But — your own . . . son!'

'Fawn is also of my blood.'

'You son of a bitch!' Nolan said scathingly and a rifle barrel cracked across his shins. Straightening, he still looked at Wolf. 'You set me after those two white men, knowing I'd kill them! And they'd done nothing! Just happened to stop by the camp! Abby even gave them biscuits!'

Wolf shrugged. 'Two less to fight Indians.'

178

'Goddamn you, Wolf! You treacherous — '

'No-lan, I once said you had some Indian ways. I wish now you were with me instead of these two.' He gestured to Bodie and McAlpine, ignoring their scowls. 'But gold would never make you turn against your own kind.'

Nolan's tone was bleak. 'They're not my kind — they're scum.' The deserters beat him down with their rifles and when Geary tried to interfere Bodie hit him so hard that he was knocked cold.

'Long as you pay what we agreed, old man,' McAlpine told Wolf, 'we'll get along. Don't mean we have to like each other. Maybe we'll up the ante, you keep on bad-mouthin' us . . . '

Wolf did not know the expression but he knew it meant that the two deserters were angry. As he still had a good deal of use for them he tried to placate them.

'You will be paid as agreed — in gold.'

'*Our* gold,' Nolan said, eyes narrowed. 'Mine and Bob's! Damn you, Wolf!'

Wolf almost smiled. 'It is good, this way. You were once with Custer, No-lan, found our camps for him, led him to his massacres! Now your gold will help . . . atone?'

'I'm surprised you've got any left.' Nolan swung an arm in the direction of the encampment. 'You've made this into a damn fine-looking reservation.'

Wolf smiled crookedly.

'With *your* gold! You would be surprised if you knew how much was spent, No-lan. And on what!'

Nolan waited but Wolf made no explanation and the two deserters were not forthcoming.

'OK, Wolf. What're we gonna do with 'em?' McAlpine was impatient. 'If there're lawmen prowlin' around, be best to get rid of 'em.'

Wolf nodded without hesitation. 'But they must not be found anywhere near the reservation,' he said slowly.

Bodie grinned, showing a couple of gaps amongst the yellowed teeth still remaining.

'Know just the place! Nice and quiet and miles from anywhere . . . '

'It must be . . . thorough,' Wolf warned. Bodie and McAlpine exchanged glances. Both men chuckled.

'Oh, it will be, Wolf, ol' hoss, it sure as hell *will* be!' McAlpine assured him. 'Thorough as all hell!'

They waited ten minutes or more after Wolf had left before they started in on Nolan again. Geary was still out to it but earned himself a couple of gratuitous kicks as Bodie and McAlpine closed in on Nolan.

They were playing with him, letting him back up and move around a little. Then they rushed him from both sides.

And got the surprise of their lives when Nolan dropped flat, rolled and somersaulted, came up behind them and butted McAlpine in the back, slammed Bodie across the neck with a hammerblow. The killers went down, McAlpine to his knees, looking grey-faced, Bodie stumbling to one knee, half-choked.

Nolan kicked him in the chest and clubbed McAlpine on the back of the neck with a closed fist. The man sprawled and, panting, Nolan snatched the Colt from McAlpine's holster. He stepped back, cocking the hammer.

'Take your time, gents.'

Through their pain the two glared hatred at him, but their eyes were focused on the gun. Nolan waited, ready to close and finish it permanently if he had to.

Then he stiffened as he felt the unmistakable pressure of a gun barrel against his spine. No one said anything, though Bodie grinned and McAlpine gave a small chuckle. Nolan slowly lowered the Colt's hammer, let the gun fall as he raised his hands, turning slowly.

He started in shock when he saw Abby holding a brand-new Winchester; he knew from past experience that she could handle a rifle well. The killers stood. McAlpine picked up his gun and strode to Nolan, spun him by the shoulder and raised the pistol to gun-whip him.

'No!' Abby snapped, the Winchester now covering McAlpine.

He and Bodie stared.

'We'll take over now, sweetheart,' said Bodie. 'You go back to the agency. He's ours.'

'Get on your horses and ride over to that flat rock. Sit there with your hands on the saddle horns where I can see you. You can come back when I say.'

They wanted to argue but there was determination and a coldness in her beautiful face that made them obey in the end. She watched them sit their mounts stiffly on the flat rock, hands where she had ordered, then turned her dark eyes to Nolan.

'I wanted to see you one more time, Matthew.'

'Didn't know you cared,' he said bitterly.

'You have lost weight — you are skinny now, but I see a lot of stringy muscle. Prison diet agrees with you.'

'You must try it some time.'

She smiled faintly but the gun didn't waver.

'No thank you. You know by now that we have put your gold to good use.'

'Not from where I'm standing.'

'Of course not. But you have no say in the matter.'

'You're a thief — and some kinda murderer if you count those two innocent whites I killed for you.'

She shrugged, utterly indifferent.

'They were . . . convenient. In a way, I'm sorry it worked out this way. As Wolf has said, you are one of the better whites, but you led Custer to our villages! My family was slaughtered. Custer and his murderers are dead. You were the one within reach and even had the means which we could use to take our revenge.'

'Thought that was still to come.'

Her eyes narrowed. 'Yes, you always could think ahead to the logical conclusion! Well, I just wanted to make sure you understood how we were using you. It's important to me that you know we have won!' She didn't move her gaze from him but raised her voice. 'You can come back now!'

McAlpine and Bodie started their mounts instantly, riding fast.

'Goodbye, Matthew.'

'*Adios*, Abby. Can't say it's been a pleasure.'

'There were . . . moments.' Her sly smile surprised him, then McAlpine put his mount between him and the girl and loosened a boot from the stirrup, kicking Nolan alongside the jaw.

Nolan collapsed, unconscious.

McAlpine looked challengingly at her but she merely lowered the rifle and said: '*Now* you can take over.'

She turned and walked away without once looking back as the men dismounted and moved in on Nolan and Geary who was just beginning to stir.

10

Unmarked Graves

Nolan had almost forgotten the desert existed. He had crossed it once when serving with Custer, but he had thought he remembered it being north of Elk Mountain. There was one far-off monumental rock that he recognized — a spire of weathered granite that vaguely resembled a cannon standing on end and, naturally, was named Gun Rock.

But it was a long, long way off, across trackless and waterless wastes.

The deserters had chosen an ideal place to kill them, leave them to the desert sands blowing in the furnace-breath wind to bury them both in unmarked graves.

Geary looked apprehensively at Nolan as both men were toppled unceremoniously from their mounts, hands now tied behind their backs. Bodie snatched up the reins and led the animals back towards the distant line of lava rocks which they had left before riding out on to the alkali.

McAlpine had his rifle in hand and grinned as he fired a series of shots at the bound men lying on their sides. Bullets showered them with stinging grains of sand and alkali. They writhed instinctively, trying to dodge. McAlpine laughed.

'On your feet, you sonuvers! You got some walkin' to do before we finish you. Might have us a little fun, too. My lesson ain't till just before sundown.'

Nolan felt his interest sharpen, despite his predicament, wondering what McAlpine had let slip. But it wouldn't matter what the killer revealed now, because he knew Nolan and Geary were dead men already. The actual killing was just a formality.

McAlpine prodded them along, walking his horse close to them, forcing them to jog-trot so as to avoid being ridden down. It amused him, and twice he kicked Nolan between the shoulders, sending him sprawling. Nolan managed to escape the hoofs but figured that sooner or later he would be trampled. He had been fighting his bonds ever since his hands had been tied behind his back at the reservation. The skin was rubbed raw on his wrists, stung by the sweat, and now the fine sand and powdery alkali made it much worse so that he had to grit his teeth against the pain.

He didn't think he had made even the smallest progress but he kept it up, twisting his hands this way and that, straining against the sweat-wet fibres of the hemp, forcing the smallest amount of stretch. Because of the way McAlpine was behaving Bodie came riding back fast and eager, after leaving their mounts amongst the lava rocks. Nolan figured he would die still trying to find the slack he needed. But there was no other hope. He couldn't make out whether Geary was doing the same. The man had been pretty damn quiet since being knocked out by the rifle butt earlier.

McAlpine suddenly reined up and angled his rifle in Nolan's direction.

'How fast can you run, Nolan? Can you beat Geary?' The man laughed as Bodie rode up, looking puzzled. 'Just tryin' to organize a race between these two.'

Bodie nodded eagerly enough.

'Why the hell not? We been waitin' a long time to get 'em in this kind of bind . . . ' He nudged his mount forward, swung a kick at Nolan's head. The man wrenched aside but the boot caught his shoulder, spun him, staggering.

It annoyed Bodie that he had missed target. Snarling a curse, he jumped his mount forward into Nolan. The man went down with a grunt and flailing legs, body twisting violently. He spat sand and grit from between his teeth, feeling the stinging bite of the alkali on his tongue. He rolled instinctively as Bodie wrenched his mount around and raced it back at him. He was on his knees, flung himself sideways and sprawled again.

'Hey, Bode? You're losin' your touch! Hell, that young Injun squaw at Rattle Crick was like a rubber ball the way you made your hoss kick her all over that field . . . '

'Had a better hoss then!' Bodie gritted, raking savagely at his horse's flanks with his spurs. They came away with dripping rowels and the horse shrilled in protest, jumped at Nolan like a log hitting the whitewater.

Nolan caught a shoulder full force on his upper body and he was hurled and tumbled three yards, bouncing off the crest of a tiny rise, alkali showering around him like a bomb exploding. He rolled and skidded down the far side, ended up on his back, face bloody, grit sticking to it, filling his mouth. But his eyes were mostly clear and he watched Bodie fight the bleeding horse — and felt the sharp flintrock under his hands. The survival adrenaline fed his reflexes instantly, and he started rubbing the wrist ropes while still lying there, arcing his body, writhing as if in pain to cover the desperate sawing at the ropes.

Luckily both killers were having their fun with Geary now. Bob was on his feet, stumbling and staggering, McAlpine and Bodie co-operating as they drove him from one to the other, trying to crush him between the horses.

'Come on, Bode!' snarled McAlpine, wheeling on the frantically dodging Geary. 'Nail the bastard! I want to hear his ribs crackin' — just like mine did when they threw us down them saloon stairs!'

'Close in then!' Bodie yelled. 'You're too far back!'

McAlpine had been trying to keep one eye on the injured Nolan, swore now, and turned back to Geary. *Get this son of a bitch mashed first*, he thought. *Then take our time to finish Nolan* . . .

Geary ran to the small rise and flung himself over the top in a desperate move, tumbling and somersaulting awkwardly. McAlpine, savagely angry because the man had ducked *underneath* his ramming horse, brought his rifle around and down, triggering. Geary's body jerked and twisted and then Nolan came surging up out of a welter of sand and alkali, snatching at the killer's smoking rifle with bloody hands.

It caught McAlpine completely unawares. The rifle was jerked from his grip before he knew what was happening. It was already cocked for his next shot at Geary. Nolan coldly drove a bullet deep into the ribcage of the panting horse. McAlpine yelped and started to throw a leg over the saddle horn as the animal started down, its heart shattered.

Bodie reined aside, just as startled, fumbled his grip on his own rifle — and by then Nolan had levered another shell into the Winchester and fired, blasting McAlpine in mid-air, the body twisting as it fell. As McAlpine hit the ground, Nolan triggered again and the gun's last bullet took the killer in the upper chest.

He slammed back and Nolan spun towards Bodie, not yet realizing that the rifle was empty. When he did, Bodie was still wrenching his mount around, bringing his sixgun over his body and triggering. Nolan felt the burn of lead across the tricep of his left shoulder, tripped and went down. Bodie rode in — but suddenly turned aside, as Nolan launched himself at McAlpine's still, bloody body, wrenching at the sixgun in the man's holster.

Bodie had always been the one with the yellow streak or, as he preferred to call it, 'the strongest yen for self-preservation'. He triggered as he spurred away, stretching his arm behind him, shooting without looking. Nolan's blood-slippery hands dragged McAlpine's Colt from the holster and he fumbled it into a two-handed grip, blasted three fast shots after the fleeing Bodie.

He saw the man jerk in the saddle, drop his revolver, then straighten and, hunched low in leather, race his mount in the direction of the distant lava. Nolan was unsteady on his feet. The blood on his mutilated hands didn't allow him to get a firm grip on the butt of the Colt. He emptied it after Bodie but the shots were wild.

Bodie, one arm dangling limply now, had no intention of making a stand: he disappeared into the heat haze. Nolan sat down with a thud, not even feeling the burning pain in his shoulder as the blood writhed down his arm, mingling with that from the rope-burns on his wrists.

Breathless, almost glare-blind now, Nolan came back to his senses minutes later, though he had had no idea of the passing time. He saw that McAlpine was dead, crawled over him to where Geary lay, hands still roped behind him. He was lying at an awkward angle and there was blood snaking from under his matted hair, dripping from one ear. He was unconscious — but he was breathing.

Gasping, Nolan lay back, squinting as he stared up at the empty, brass-coloured sky. He moaned when he saw that the sun was not yet at its zenith. A long day lay ahead!

And the whole blazing, throbbing desert encircled them. He couldn't even try to make it back to the lava-line. Bodie would set up an ambush where he would have a fine view of anything bigger than a scorpion moving out in the white, blinding alkali.

South was in the direction of the reservation, though the killers had taken trouble to bamboozle them with blindfolds and many false turns before driving them into this blinding hell. He didn't know what lay due north, but slightly west of north was Gun Rock. That other time, when he was Custer's scout, he had uncovered an Indian well hidden by flat rocks. It contained insect-laden, scummy water. The troop had been desperate enough to drink the muck, their horses, too, and it had virtually saved them all.

That was years ago, but Indians had been using the same hidden wells for hundreds of years, so maybe there would be water of some sort still in the hole . . . if he could find it again.

Then he remembered McAlpine's dead horse. The man's canteen would be there! Making a strange sound in the back of his throat, he crawled towards the carcass, which had already attracted a cloud of black flies seemingly out of nowhere.

Before he reached it, he stopped, sat back and felt something drain out of him — just as the water was draining out of the bullet-punctured canteen caught half-beneath the carcass of the horse.

★   ★   ★

Nolan stripped the dead McAlpine; the man no longer had any use for his clothes or anything else, but Nolan did.

He tore strips off the shirt, soaked them in the few drops of water remaining in a corner of the battered canteen and cleaned up Geary's head wound. It wasn't deep but coming on top of his being knocked-out by the rifle butt, it had put him into a deep coma-like sleep.

Nolan knew they had a long, long walk ahead of them if they were to reach water — at least the only place he knew that *might* still hold hidden water out here. He used McAlpine's knife to cut the seams of the corduroy trousers, made two crude capes that they would be able to drape around head and shoulders. The saddle flaps he shaped into half-face masks, made slits where the eyes would be. The small openings would cut the glare and help save their vision. He made thongs to hold the masks in place. Out here, preserving your sight was just as important — or more so in some ways — than finding water. With matted, infected eyes, most likely fly-blown, a man couldn't even tell which way he was headed.

Taking stock, he found they had food for a couple of days, but it was mostly jerked or salted meat and would only increase their raging thirsts. He would take it along, but would try to refrain from eating it until they had water. A man could survive longer without food than water, anyway.

It was a pity to waste all that horsemeat but it couldn't be helped. He had rigged shade for Geary and now had to wait for the man to come round. He couldn't carry him, but could help him along once he was on his feet. There was ammunition for the sixgun, taken from McAlpine's belt, and he searched for and recovered the Colt dropped by Bodie.

So they had food, guns for protection and shade for now. If they could find water, anywhere, they would eventually survive, he was sure of it. He sat back to wait for Geary to come round, rummaged again in the saddle-bags, looking for tobacco. He found a little in a linen sack but no papers. He took out what he had thought were some letters in the bottom of McAlpine's bag, folded and grubby from much handling or simply from riding in the leather bags. But when he opened them out, intending to tear off enough to roll a smoke, he paused, frowning.

There were diagrams on both pages. It took him a short time before he recognized the first page as being sketches of attack strategies on a column of soldiers. But the second page he knew right away.

It was how to assemble a Gatling gun, — with instructions on how to fire and maintain the weapon.

11

Gun Rock

The night was a blessing in one way because the sun wasn't blasting down and blistering every inch of skin that was exposed — the backs of their hands, their necks and the tops of their chests where their shirts were open. Neither man had a neckerchief and the crude capes had no collars to pull up for protection. The tips of their noses, lips, chins, all were burned.

The night was also cool — and, later, *cold*. Colder than Nolan remembered, for it was years since he had been in desert country this far north. Geary was still a little off balance, complaining of headaches, sore ears and double vision. But Nolan knew they were much better off for wearing the improvised sun masks: without them they both would be glare-blind by now, out of their heads with pain and the fear of encroaching total blindness.

Thirst was with them to stay, it seemed. They could not make saliva now: the best they could produce was little white balls that resembled cotton — and were just as dry. Lips were cracked and blistered already, lower faces dusted with alkali. They were not pretty creatures, what with their ragged, improvised capes hanging from slumped shoulders, shirts and trousers stiff with alkali dust and sweat. They spoke only rarely, then briefly.

Moving in slow motion, they scooped out hollows in the desert and pulled a layer of warm sand over them.

'Bit deeper'd save us trouble in the long run,' whispered Geary hoarsely. Nolan forced a short laugh. 'Think I'd like my grave a mite more comfortable.'

'Like with a barrel of water built in!'

Nolan's chuckle was genuine this time: it was a good sign, Geary retaining his sense of humour.

'Glad you're feeling better, Bob.'

'Who's feelin' better? I feel like *hell*!'

'Know what you mean. Tomorrow we ought to reach Gun Rock.'

'You think we — can — crawl on this stuff?' Geary tried to spit but was unsuccessful and began to cough, clutching his chest. When the bout had finished, he gasped. 'Judas! That hurt!'

'Yeah. We've breathed in plenty of alkali. See if we can get some sleep, Bob. We're gonna need it.'

Geary grunted and Nolan settled, trying to get in the mood for sleep. But his mind was racing. What if there was no water at Gun Rock? Well, they'd be no worse off than now, except they could settle down to waiting until they were worse off, which would be inevitable . . . and very final.

He was too blamed tired and feeling too bad to try to rouse himself into more positive thoughts. Dying of thirst wasn't anything to look forward to. Of course, they had a loaded gun each. They could . . .

By hell, no! That roused him, scared him, that he was slipping so quickly into thoughts of suicide. He *must* be feeling low! All right! Tomorrow they *would* find water at Gun Rock! If they didn't . . .

Then they would keep going until they did find it! Even as he began to slip slowly into a kind of doze, he realized it was only a psychological boost.

There was nowhere else in this hellish place where they could look for water. Nowhere at all!

★   ★   ★

Barney Wales wasn't happy about Dakota Case taking charge.

The small size of the man irked him for one thing, but what stuck in his craw most was the fact that Case had beaten him to the draw, thereby making him kingpin. So their ride down from Elk Mountain and back to Longbow was mostly in silence.

But when they came in sight of the scattered buildings of the distant Longbow, Case turned to the sullen Wales and spoke to him.

'You're a strange man, Wales.'

The sheriff said nothing to that, made no sign he had even heard.

'You suddenly appear on the lawman scene with a ready-made reputation: fast, deadly and a real heller — *you* say.'

Barney looked at him now, eyes dark and flashing.

'I *am* a real heller, mister. You'd do well to remember that.'

Dakota nodded slowly.

'Think you're right. There is a deeper side to you than you let show.'

For a moment, Wales's face tightened, but then he relaxed it, forced a casual shrug of his big shoulders.

'I ain't gonna lose any sleep over what you think — or don't think.'

'Fair enough. But there's a story about you destroying a lot of Wanted dodgers that had your name on 'em. If it's true, you must be a man who's dumped his past and turned to punchin' law in a kind of repentance. I can admire such a man. But if it ain't true, I'd have to wonder like hell why any man would start such a rumour in the first place.'

'Told you, don't care what you think.'

'OK, I can be comfortable with that. Just tell me one thing: you ever in the army?'

Barney frowned. 'The hell makes you ask that?'

'Just the way you carry yourself sometimes. When you ain't working at slouching around like a gorilla I see a touch of army ramrod in your back that any man who's had it planted there can never quite get rid of.'

'Well, you got a sharp eye. I fought in the war, start to finish. Drifted after, broke mostly, then decided the country owed me some kinda livin', joined the cavalry but . . . ' He shrugged. 'We didn't see eye to eye.'

'I can read as much or as little into that as I like, Barney!'

'And welcome to do it! Hell with you, Case!' Wales rammed his heels into his mount's flanks and spurred on ahead towards the town.

Case scrubbed a hand around his stubbled jowls, then urged his mount into a jog-trot, lips pursed thoughtfully.

★　★　★

There was no water at Gun Rock.

Or, if there was, Nolan couldn't find it. He tried to recall how it had looked years earlier when Custer had been riding him ragged to locate water for the troop. It was hard to bring back a picture from those times, but he found he could visualize it if he made himself concentrate.

Now the place was grey and depressing, the silence broken only by the mournful moaning of wind through eroded holes in the flared base of the rock pinnacle. There were flat slabs of shale, splintered far back in the ages before man walked this part of the earth. Slabs stood on end, lay scattered about, some too big for any man to handle alone. None of them looked like the ones he had located covering the old Indian well.

'Might be round the other side,' grated Geary hoarsely.

Nolan frowned, rubbed his gritty forehead, head throbbing like a war-dance drum.

'No-o, don't think so. Custer brought us in across the south corner of the desert so we would've come up on this side . . . '

'You sure?' Geary pointed with an arm that trembled, the shirt-sleeve ragged, heavy with accumulated alkali and sand. 'That sparklin' place down there looks like flint to me. Even Custer wouldn't be fool enough to lead mounted soldiers across that. He'd skirt it and that'd bring him out — well, take your pick of the whole opposite side.'

Nolan had to think about it. He found it hard to run even two or three thoughts together and knew he was near exhaustion. He had carried Geary over his shoulder for a couple of miles and the wounded man seemed quite lucid now. He thought about what Bob had said, then slowly nodded.

'Think you're right. I got some recollection of it. We got nothing to lose by lookin', anyway.'

They dragged themselves around the broken base of the towering rock, stumbling and falling, staggering, gasping, feeling their throats gradually closing and cutting down the air they sucked into their lungs. Both men were sweating and down on hands and knees when Nolan recognized the area. He tried to grin but his lips split and oozed blood. He couldn't speak, his tongue was swollen too much. But he pointed to a series of slabs, each only a few feet square and not too thick . . .

It took them an hour of muscle-cracking, gasping effort moving several of these before they eventually uncovered the Indian well.

The well smelled putrid, water dark

brown, scummed with dead leaves and twigs and insects — but the insects were living: small water-beetles skimming the surface. Nolan started to climb down, slipped and fell. He landed knee-deep in the liquid, sucking ooze underfoot, and, unable to stop himself, driven by a thirst of an intensity he had never known before, he scooped up a handful and filled his mouth.

He spat beetles and berries and other rubbish, but swallowed some. It had no taste to his traumatized taste-buds or gullet. But it was wet — *wet* and soothing. He coughed, waved weakly to Geary.

'Champagne!' he croaked, and Geary started down immediately . . .

Later, sitting in the shade of the big rock, bellies sloshing — and feeling a little queasy — they grinned at each other, savouring the moment. Then Nolan remembered the little bit of tobacco he had found, took it from his shirt pocket and brought out the papers he had taken from the bottom of

McAlpine's saddle-bags.

He started to tear off enough to roll a cigarette which they would share, when he stopped and looked at the sketches on the grimy page again. He lifted reddened eyes to Geary.

'Bob, you recollect just what Bodie and McAlpine did before they deserted?'

Geary frowned, trying to sort out his thoughts.

'Well, they weren't in our troop. They were in the second troop, I think. Why?'

'That was artillery, wasn't it? Cannon and . . . Gatling guns?'

Bob snorted. 'We only had one of *them*! And it disappeared about the time Bodie and McAlpine deserted. Recollect Custer, always tryin' to cover himself, said they must've stole it and sold it to the Injuns. Give 'em a stake and getaway money so's they could hide from the army.'

'And they were never caught for desertion,' Nolan added thoughtfully. 'Wonder how those two made a living and stayed outta sight?'

'We know they were claim-jumpers. And guns for hire.'

'Sure. But what else? Someone must've been hiding them. In exchange for . . . what?'

Geary stiffened. 'Maybe . . . someone . . . wanted to learn how to use a Gatling gun,' he suggested slowly.

12

Longbow

Monte Wales was waiting when Dakota Case and Barney rode into Longbow.

'The hell're you doin' here, l'il brother?' Barney demanded, making it clear he wasn't pleased to see Monte and so annoyed that he missed the worried look on his younger brother's face. But Case noticed.

'What's up, Monte?'

'They escaped,' the Cheyenne sheriff said flatly, with a touch of bitterness.

'Who?' blurted Barney. 'Not Nolan and . . . '

Monte nodded jerkily. 'Both of 'em.'

'Christ almighty! How the hell did that happen? Figured I'd taught you better'n that! Goddamnit, I spent years tryin' to teach you how to do things *right*! Now — '

'What happened, Monte?' Case asked in a quieter voice.

The younger Wales shrugged, resignation partially covering the shame that was eating at him.

'Somehow they sweet-talked Lucille, got her to open Nolan's cell door.' He looked embarrassed.

'Damn women!' grated Barney, almost spitting. 'Don't matter how old they are, a man flatters 'em and they go all droopy and do anythin' he wants! Thank Christ I never married!'

'Shut up, Barney, no one'd have the likes of you, anyway,' Case snapped, turning to Monte. 'She all right, son?'

'They locked her in but didn't hurt her. Then, when they hightailed it they shot out three insulators on the telegraph line so I couldn't send you a message. I just rode two hosses into the ground gettin' here to warn you.'

Case eased back his hat and scratched his head.

'Well, if they were headin' this way, I'd say they were makin' for Elk Mountain.'

'Nothin' surer!' snapped the angry Barney Wales, moving impatiently from one foot to the other. 'They're goin' after that damn gold!'

'Well, they figure it belongs to 'em,' Case said reasonably, 'but they won't have no more luck than we did. They'll be headin' for the reservation, all right, might've already been there and gone. There's been time enough.'

Barney dragged a horny fingernail through his sand-clogged beard stubble.

'Possible. Could've even been there same time as us!' That thought didn't please him and he swore softly. 'Well, it's gettin' dark. Might's well stay over night, get some decent grub and a rest, then get after 'em come mornin'.'

Case frowned and shook his head.

'Not me. I'll have to get back to Laramie. I don't run to a deputy on my budget and I been away long enough.' He flicked his gaze to Barney. 'On a wild-goose chase,' he added.

'The hell you mean, 'wild-goose chase'? There's gold, all right! You take an Injun's word when he says he knows nothin' about it?' The big sheriff looked and sounded disgusted but Case seemed unfazed.

'Already told you. That's Federal land up there. It'll take a US marshal with a warrant to get anywhere — and even then I don't like his chances.'

'Well, you worry about Federal warrants all you want, Dakota. I didn't come all this way and done the things I've done just to leave that gold to a bunch of Injuns!'

'For crying out loud, man, how much d'you think is left after all this time? You said yourself it was a top-notch reservation and must've had plenty spent on it.'

Barney looked bleak. 'I heard Nolan and Geary talkin' between themselves in my cell-block. They didn't know anyone could hear down that passage. They said they worked their butts off for that gold in the Sonora rush, heaps of it, and that blamed squaw and her old man stole it from them! It exists, all right, and I'm goin' after it!'

Case shrugged. 'Suit yourself. But I have to get back to Laramie. I wish you luck.'

'I'll come with you, Barney,' said Monte. His elder brother smiled crookedly.

'Don't really believe in it, but you'd like a share just the same, eh, kid?'

'I'm comin' because there're two prisoners out there that escaped from my jail and I aim to bring 'em back.' Monte's young face hardened, as did his voice. 'Nothin's gonna get in the way of me doin' that, Barney — includin' a burro-load of gold.'

Barney managed to keep the hard, stubborn look on his face, but he was a mite uneasy inside. He'd never figured the kid was that devoted to his badge.

Maybe he had taught him a little *too* well and now it was coming home to roost.

*   *   *

Barney was in a sour mood as he walked through the early-morning streets of Longbow, smelling breakfasts cooking as smoke curled from chimney-stacks. He hadn't slept well. *Too damn much on my mind*, he told himself, and he was probably right.

Monte could be a nuisance coming with him, so if he could clear town without him all the better. He turned into the livery and slowed, frowning.

At the far end of the aisle the hostler was checking over two horses, a sorrel and a chestnut, and both seemed to have *grey legs*. That was queer, and Barney went forward, puzzled. The hostler glanced up.

'Just about to ask you how come them broncs had grey legs but now I'm closer I can see they ain't grey — just dusted with alkali.'

The hostler grunted, hitched at his baggy coveralls and went back to examining the horses' feet.

'Feller come in all dusted the same way — wants to sell me these here.'

'Where is he?'

The hostler jerked his head towards a stall to Barney's left. Barney turned, stepped inside as he saw a man watching him warily over the back of a long-legged black. He was washing aklali from the glistening coat.

'Been doin' some desert travellin'?' Barney asked casually, not missing the man's tension now he had seen Wales's badge.

'Just cuttin' across the west corner.'

'Wouldn't pick up all that alkali just crossin' that part. You been through the middle.'

The man shrugged. 'Mebbe.'

'So why lie?' Barney squinted. 'Say — I know you?'

'Don't think so. Name's Bodine.'

Barney smiled thinly. 'Reckon you mean 'Bodie'. Where's McAlpine?'

Bodie stiffened, ran a tongue over sun-scorched lips, glanced past Barney's shoulder and saw another man enter the livery — and the low-slanting sun glinted off a badge on *his* vest, too!

Bodie swore, punched the black in the genitals and the horse's rear legs sagged as it whickered and plunged. Bodie pushed it towards Barney Wales.

The deserter's gun hammered as he lunged for the exit of the stall, knocking Wales aside. Barney hit the wall, his own gun coming up, blasting splinters from the opposite wall as Bodie stumbled out into the aisle. The hostler was running for cover and the two mounts that had belonged to Nolan and Geary snorted and plunged, blocking his escape in that direction.

Then one lunged away, slamming Bodie aside, charging down on Monte who had walked right into this, suspecting earlier that Barney might try to ride out without him. He brought up his gun and triggered, his shot making Bodie stagger but the man fired twice and Monte, intent on dodging the running horse as it charged past, went down to sprawl in the aisle.

Barney, out of the stall now after

slamming his gun across the head of the spooked black, saw Bodie running for it, leaping over Monte. The big sheriff steadied the Colt in both hands, aimed carefully and fired. Bodie went down on the run, skidding along through the straw and manure, losing his pistol as he brought up short against Monte's still form.

Barney, limping some, was standing above him in seconds, smoking Colt pointing down into the sweating, fear-ridden face. Eyes bulging, Bodie lifted a dirty hand in vain protection.

'Don't!' he croaked.

'Aw, don't worry, Bodie. You an' me're due for a little talk. I need to know what you're doin' with Nolan's and Geary's hosses and a few other things. Go to sleep for now.'

Barney gunwhipped the man solidly in the head, then knelt beside Monte. The younger Wales was gasping for breath, blood oozing between the fingers of the hand he pressed into the left side of his chest.

'You — killed him!' he said, looking at the stilled Bodie.

'Nah! His head's solid bone. Wouldn't even feel it. Stay put, l'il brother — I'll get a sawbones . . . '

He moved towards a group of early risers who were crowding into the livery now.

'Someone send for the doc and hurry it up!'

★   ★   ★

Bodie had lost a lot of blood, the mattress on the narrow cot in the rear of the doctor's infirmary was soaked red. There were bloody rags on the floor and Bodie held another awkwardly against his back low down on the left side.

'You — you didn't bust my . . . kidney, did you?' he asked in a croaking voice as Barney sniffed and sat on the edge of a straightback chair, pulling it in close to the cot.

'Not yet.'

Bodie was an awful colour, a mixture of purple, grey and yellow, but his face blanched at Barney's words.

'I — I want the sawbones!'

'He's busy with my kid brother. I'm lookin' after you till he gets time to take care of you.'

'No! No, I don't want you! I want — the doc!'

He tried to sit up and Barney thrust him back roughly.

'You just lie there and take it easy. You got a lot of talking to do — and there's plenty of time! I can guarantee the sawbones won't come in here till I call him. You savvy, Bodie?'

'Aw, Christ!'

Wales shook his head, lifting his hands and flexing his big fingers.

'He won't help you. There's just you and me, Bodie. Now let me get you comfortable.'

He reached one hand under Bodie and clamped the other over the man's mouth as he started to scream. Bodie's eyes bulged like peeled chestnuts and he convulsed as the terrible pain racked his body . . .

Barney walked into the doctor's operating-room, wiping his bloody hands on a rag. The doctor's wife was mopping down a narrow operating-table and the doctor, gaunt and grim, was washing his bloodstained hands in carbolic water. He glared at Barney, who only had eyes for the pale Monte lying on a narrow bed, his chest swathed in clean bandages.

'Hope you got better news for me than I've got for you, Doc.'

'What the devil does that mean? If you've harmed that patient in there — '

'Never mind him, Doc. Tell me about my brother.'

The medic continued to glare, rinsed his hands and began to dry them on a towel.

'Well, he'll pull through, but he's going to be laid up for some time. I've dug out the bullet so there's little chance of infection now and it didn't touch any major organs — pure luck, I suspect. But he'll need a lot of bed-rest.'

'Send the bill to me.'

'Gladly! Where will the undertaker send his bill? For that man Bodie.'

'Aw, you think he won't make it, Doc? Well, you could be right. No loss to anyone. Bad sonuver, army deserter, killer, thief, spoiler of young women . . . '

'As you say, no loss, but he is still a human being and I took an oath to heal. I should never have let you intimidate me! Bodie was the more seriously injured but you insisted I work on this man first!'

'My kid brother, Doc. Remember what I said? If you didn't give him priority or somethin' happened to him, I was gonna crush your fingers one by one with my gunbutt . . . '

The doctor was very pale now, licked his lips.

'I — believed you! Courage is not one of my — attributes. But I suspect I may've capitulated a little too quickly . . . '

Barney smiled thinly. 'You can still use your hands, doc. Be thankful. I've got places to go, but I'll be back to check on my brother. So take good care of him.'

'He asked that you send a wire to his wife, let her know he'll be some time recovering.'

'Good to know they've fixed the line. Yeah, I'll be glad to wire Lucille. Got some messages to send myself. Much obliged, Doc. I'll just turn up when I get a chance.'

Barney waved as he went out and the medic's body slumped in relief as he said quietly,

'Don't hurry on my account, you sadistic, murdering swine!'

Barney didn't hear him but even if he had, the doctor knew the man would have merely laughed, highly amused.

13

The Army Never Forgets

With the food, cooked over a fire mostly made from dried twigs found jammed in the sides of the well, together with some slivers of wood shaved from the rifle stock for kindling, and the water, now being strained through a shirt, Nolan and Geary felt as if they were once again back in the land of the living.

The sunburn still hurt and so did their wounds, but their bellies were full and they were able to wash away the salty taste of the bacon with water the colour of weak coffee but mostly clear. They even squeezed the residue of mud and dead insects remaining in the shirt material and saved a few more precious drops of liquid.

They smoked the last of the tobacco

in a match-slim cigarette and once again Nolan spread out what was left of the papers he had taken from McAlpine's saddlebags.

'This is a plan of attack, I guess,' he said, his voice not so hoarse now. He indicated the paper with a lot of crude horses and man-drawings. 'See the way the curved arrows sweep in and around, like pincers? And this here big cross with the gun on wheels must be the Gatling's position.'

Geary still had a thundering headache and rubbed above his right eye as he squinted at the papers.

'Yeah. Readin' it as a lay-out, the attack would have to be in a kind of basin, the Gatling set high, waiting for the Indians to drive the soldiers into the trap. Be like shootin' fish in a barrel.'

Nolan nodded. 'McAlpine was a sergeant. Bodine a corporal. They'd know something of military tactics, more than the troopers . . . ' He held up the drawings of the Gatling gun and its straight-feed magazines. 'My guess is

Bodie and McAlpine were hired by Black Wolf to teach his warriors how to shoot the Gatling and maintain it — their magazines are notorious for jamming up with powder and the spring-feed has always given trouble. They'd know how to correct that.'

Geary frowned again. 'Reckon Injuns would be able to grasp it?'

'Why not? Mechanics might be strange to 'em but they're just as smart as anyone else, commonsense-wise.'

Geary shook his head slowly, regretting the movement.

'Can't savvy any white man helpin' Injuns to slaughter other whites.'

'They're not the first and won't be the last. Question is, what do we do about it? Or, what *can* we do about it, stuck out here?'

'There's the big army post at Fort McFadden — thirty miles away, I know. And we're afoot. And dunno when they plan the attack anyways.'

'Or even whether one is planned. We're pretty damn sure from this but you know the army. They'd take a lot of convincing before they'd move in on an Indian reservation after the slaughter that took place to avenge Custer's massacre.'

Geary shrugged and wearily leaned back against Gun Rock, looking at the sun climbing towards the zenith.

'Well, we're stuck here for a spell, anyway.'

Nolan's wolfish face was grim but he nodded gently. 'Looks that way. If it was anyone else but Wolf, I wouldn't let it bother me, but that old sonuver hates whites like a preacher hates sin — worse! He lost two families to Custer's raids on their camps, Abby told me. Horse Catcher's mother and sisters, then Abby's mother and a kid brother a few years later.' He flicked his gaze to Geary's interested face. 'That last was up on the Milk River, place called . . . '

'Not Reedy Bend!' Geary said gaspingly. 'Judas, we were there! You scouted and I was in charge of 'B'

Troop! And Custer gave his usual order: 'Kill 'em all!' Hell, you think Wolf knew that? And that's why he took our gold? Sort of — we pay for helpin' wipe out his family, by financin' this mad attack he's workin' on! Christ, Matt! It could be that way!'

'Yeah, Abby said something like that, Bob. Wolf couldn't've planned on using us, but when we showed up in Buckeye and I went after Abby — I had the feeling that he was laughing at me all along. Using me, and me too dumb to see it or do anything about it! All I could see was Abby!'

Geary sighed. 'Well, whatever's behind it, we can't do a damn thing from out here — unless you know how to grow a set of wings, maybe?'

Nolan scowled. 'Seems the only way, don't it.'

But the fatigue from the desert crossing, together with the food, soon overwhelmed them, and they slept.

* * *

When they opened their eyes Big Barney Wales was sitting on a rock, smoking, watching them, a rifle in his lap. They started to struggle up.

'Just stay put a minute, gents. You two got more lives than a witch's cat!'

Beyond him they could see four horses ground-hitched on a slab of rock. One was Wales's own mount, a black with a white arc above his left eye, another was a shag-coated pack-horse, and the other two were Nolan's and Geary's mounts, saddled, with canteens hung from the horns, rifles in the scabbards.

'What's going on, Barney?' Geary asked, blinking.

'How did you get here?' Nolan asked before Wales could answer.

'Aw, me and Bodie had a little . . . talk. He was afraid of dyin' and wanted to clear his conscience so he told me a lot more'n I bargained on. He died anyway.'

Geary and Nolan exchanged glances but said nothing.

'Seen those papers you left weighted down with a stone yonder. Gatling gun diagrams and what looks like an attack plan for driving a lot of men into an ambush.'

'Got 'em from McAlpine's saddle-bags.'

'Un-huh. You figured 'em out?'

Nolan told him briefly what they thought had happened and Barney smiled crookedly, nodding.

'Yeah, you'd be smart enough to see it. Bodie and McAlpine supplied the Gatling gun and a lot of new repeatin' rifles they stole from armouries around the country. How they been makin' a livin' since they deserted, Injuns hidin' 'em out. That's where most of your gold went, payin' for guns. Accordin' to Bodie, Wolf's about ready to make his move. Gonna hit the monthly patrol from Fort McFadden.'

Bob whistled through his teeth. Nolan asked, 'Where?'

'Work it out. By the bend of the big river — plain as day on that sketch of the attack. Din' you figure that?'

'No, I hadn't,' Nolan admitted, 'but I can see it now you mention it. Hit 'em on the bend where the sand and gravel is deep and loose, to slow the horses down. Come through the cutting and the soldiers would naturally cross the river because it's shallow there, but forced by the cliffs on the other side to ride only one way . . . '

'Into Pinchgut Canyon,' Wales said with a touch of triumph. 'Name says it all. They come in through the bottleneck and the Gatling's perched on a ledge, a hundred screamin' warriors behind. Little Big Horn all over again.'

Nolan squinted at the big, hard-faced sheriff.

'Know when?'

'Patrol's already on the way to the riverbend. Left yesterday.'

'Judas! We'll have to warn 'em!' Geary said, standing and swaying as a wave of dizziness hit him. He steadied himself against a rock.

'Been done.'

They stared at Wales and he shrugged. 'Wired the fort last night from Longbow. They'll have sent a rider after the patrol by now. He might be in time.'

'*You* warned 'em?' Nolan said slowly, watching Wales's impassive face. 'Why? You won't get anything out of it. The gold's mostly gone by now, like you say, maybe all of it. Wolf'd rather have killed Bodie and McAlpine instead of paying 'em is my guess. What's in it for you?'

Wales grinned wickedly. 'You'll just have to wonder. We ain't got a lot of time if we want to see the action.'

'What action?' Geary asked.

'When the army hit Elk Mountain reservation and wipe Wolf's tribe off the map!'

Nolan went very still. 'They wouldn't do that, just on the say-so of a wire from a small-town sheriff, hundreds of miles from his jurisdiction.'

'You're wastin' time!' Wales snapped, turning away towards the tethered horses.

Puzzled, and not a little worried, Nolan and Geary stumbled after the sheriff.

★   ★   ★

They were almost too late.

Almost — because something had slipped in the plan, whatever it was, and the army did not get a chance to attack the Indians on Elk Mountain. Instead, they adhered rigidly to the regular patrol route, intending to cross the river at the bend as usual, *then* swing towards the reservation. It was logical enough in its way as it was a shorter route than going around the base of the mountain to the trail leading to the top. It would also allow the troop to approach closer before it was seen by look-outs that Wolf no doubt had posted.

Barney Wales had said little on the long, hot ride out of the desert. He was leading the weary, wounded ex-miners towards the mountain by a trail that would take them about half-way between the reservation and the river bend.

That was when they heard the gunfire.

All three reined down abruptly, hipping in the saddles, staring towards the distant crackle of rifles and the popping of sixguns.

'That's comin' from the riverbend!' Nolan said and swore. 'Goddamn bone-headed army officers!'

Wales lifted his reins and jammed in his heels, abandoning the lead rope of the alkali-dusted pack-horse, reaching for his rifle. 'C'mon! We can still get into this!'

Nolan and Geary were near exhaustion, hammered by the sun, still suffering the after-effects of their wounds and yesterday's raging thirst. But they unsheathed the rifles Wales had brought for them and spurred after him.

They smelled the gunsmoke drifting through the timber before they saw the battlefield. Then it was difficult to make out many details, for the smoke hung in a thick fog, with riders dashing about wildly, everyone yelling, white men and Indians. The roaring shouts of the soldiers mingled with the higher-pitched war cries of the Sioux.

All were partly drowned out by the crash of gunfire as they rode in, Wales veering to the left, Geary to the right, leaving the straight-ahead line for Nolan. He thought: *At least the Gatling gun's not working yet!*

It would only be a matter of time, though, and he wondered if it was in position on a ledge in Pinchgut Canyon, waiting for its victims — or was it somewhere closer? Set up in that stand of timber, perhaps. Wolf would realize that something must have happened to McAlpine and Bodie when they didn't return, and that more than likely his plans had been discovered. He was smart enough to modify them to be safe.

He was a clever strategist, driven by a ruthlessness and desire for revenge that few white men would ever know — or even understand.

Nolan had no time to consider any more. A bullet clipped the brim of his hat and dust and alkali wreathed his face briefly in a mist that made him cough. The motion jerked his head and saved his life as another whipped past close enough for him to feel the scorch as it cleaved the air. He stretched out along his horse's neck, brought his rifle across his body and fired as a screaming Indian raced in, rifle spitting flame and smoke. But the Sioux was not used to a white man's weapon and his shots were wild — close, but wild — and after the third one he pitched headlong from his racing mount. Nolan was sure he heard the man's neck crack.

He wheeled away as another Sioux lunged at him with a stone-headed lance — there were always some old warriors who preferred to fight with traditional weapons, eager to face the Great Spirit, whether modern paleface guns were available or not. Nolan sent this one to his Happy Hunting Grounds with a bullet through the neck. His blood sprayed hotly across Nolan's sorrel's eyes and it swerved drunkenly in brief panic.

He found himself facing a trio of painted, screaming braves. They wheeled their mounts around him, yodelling their death songs as they brought rifles to bear on him. Nolan slid his own near-empty rifle under the saddle-flap, hanging off to one side by his left hand, body almost dragging on the ground as he drew the Colt and thumbed four shots faster than he ever could remember. Two Indians threw up their arms and pitched out of their saddles. The third's horse shuddered and staggered, whickering wildly as blood spurted from its neck. The rider jolted forward in the saddle and Nolan crashed the butt of his smoking pistol into the contorted face.

He hauled upright, holstered the Colt, and slid the rifle out again. He saw Geary smash his Winchester's barrel across the bridge of the nose of a painted warrior. The man rolled back over his horse's rump. Geary spun the rifle around the trigger-guard in a flashy though very effective action that worked the lever and jacked a shell into the chamber just as the barrel levelled on another yelling, blood-mad Sioux. The shot blew the man clear out of the saddle but the horse, mane flying, cannoned into Geary's mount and knocked him to the ground.

Two Indians swerved and ran their horses at the floundering man. Nolan jumped his sorrel forward with a screaming cry. It smashed into the closest horse, knocking it sprawling on to its side. The rider cried out as his leg was crushed beneath it. Before he could get up Nolan lowered the rifle to within three inches of his head and triggered.

He veered away after seeing Geary shoulder-roll and get up groggily, rifle trailing. He caught his mount's reins with one hand and managed to vault into the saddle. Nolan skirted him, came up with a quartet of soldiers, all of them bloodied, uniforms torn and stained.

Without a word, they lined up and all six riders charged into the seething mass of whites and red men, fighting it out at the river's edge. Water frothed and churned and was tinged with blood as guns hammered and army sabres sliced and cut, tomahawks flashed as they spun through the air and the blades found a home in some luckless trooper.

Nolan was almost deaf, his head ringing with a cacophony of noise, even the close gunfire sounding muffled.

But he heard the sudden, thundering, hammering, evenly spaced shots overwhelming the sounds of battle. Troopers were being smashed from their saddles, the ground about the feet of unhorsed men was torn and erupting as they ran. He saw a soldier's legs ripped from under him, the body shuddering and jumping wildly as heavy-calibre slugs almost cut the man in two.

He also saw the thick pall of black-tinged milky smoke spurting from among the trees.

Nolan slammed his mount ashore, dodging dead and dying men in the bloody shallows. He flung himself from the saddle, ran in a crouch to some rocks and dropped behind them. Heavy slugs chipped away at the stone briefly before moving on, tearing a spurting line across the sand, men twisting and thrashing in macabre death-throes.

His rifle reloaded, Nolan took time to reload his Colt too, ducking as someone leapt their mount over his shelter. He saw that it was Geary, in hot pursuit of a fleeing Indian. The troopers were all hunting cover now as the Gatling gun continued its devastating arcs of death . . .

In a lull — he figured whoever was manning the Gatling was having trouble switching to a full magazine — Nolan gathered himself, leapt over the rock and ran for the edge of the timber. His legs pounded in the loose sand and he stumbled twice, heart hammering, lungs bursting, the long-forgotten madness of battle now gripping him and driving him on. He had known that unseen force keep a man dead on his feet running for several yards before collapsing.

He burst through a screen of brush sooner than he expected and stumbled out into the clearing where the Gatling gun had been set up in a wagon-bed, giving it elevation and an excellent line of fire. There were four Indians there and three of them came screaming at him, one with a bow, arrow fitted, curving into an arc. The other two had guns. Nolan shot the man with the bow and he twisted with the strike of lead, loosing his arrow into the back of his nearest companion. The man screamed as he fell and Nolan dropped to one knee, shot the one armed with a rifle in the belly, spun to the arrow-wounded man who was bringing up his own rifle. Nolan's bullet tore the man's face apart, then he grunted and was borne to the ground by the gutshot warrior who now had a broad-bladed knife in his fist.

The man was already dead by the look of his eyes, but he was determined to take at least one white-eye with him when he made the final slide into Eternity. The knife plunged down, ripped Nolan's shirt and part of his shoulder, and then the white man rammed a knee into the belly wound and the red man whirled away, convulsing. He would be dead in a second and as Nolan started up, reaching for the rifle, the Gatling gun fired and he felt the hammering concussion of the explosions driving against his already tortured eardrums.

He spilled to the ground, clapping hands over his ears in agony, rolling away from the grass and dirt that erupted around him. He felt the blast of the muzzle as it tracked him, felt the ground tremble with the impact of the big .70-calibre slugs, and then he was under the wagon that supported the big gun.

Moving by instinct, he rolled out, Colt in hand. As he glimpsed the Indian gunner — Wolf — struggling to depress the muzzle enough to shoot him, Nolan fired twice. The Indian reared on to his feet and went over the raised side of the wagon, moccasins lifting briefly before he fell from sight. The first thing Nolan did was wrench the magazine off the gun and hurl it into the trees. He placed the muzzle of the sixgun bare inches from the breech and fired. The recoil made the gun jump from his hand, sending electric flashes of pain through his wrist. Metal fragments shrieked past his face. He stumbled and fell over the side, thankful that the Gatling would never fire again in this battle.

Dazed, he shook his head as he lay on his side, gasping for breath. He stiffened as he looked into the pain-contorted face of Black Wolf, who now carried two of Nolan's bullets in his body.

The mad eyes blazed and the purplish, leathery lips pulled back from his yellowed teeth.

'Kill me, No-lan. *Finish it!*'

The man was holding a hand against his torn and bloody chest and Nolan sat up, looked bleakly into the hate-filled face, raised his Colt — then shook his head slowly.

'I reckon you can pull through, Wolf. I want to see you swing high on the Cheyenne gallows. Bullet's too quick for you.'

He was unprepared for the piercing, animal scream that came from Black Wolf.

'*Kill me, you — white — scum!*'

'Sorry, Wolf. I'm out of ammo — and it looks like your men have been beaten. Those that ain't dead are surrendering. No Indian victory this time.'

Wolf was so enraged he passed out. Then Geary and Barney Wales, both blood-spattered, stained with black powdersmoke, clothes torn, came over and helped him to his feet.

As he steadied, poking a finger into his ear, working his jaws, Nolan looked up, straight at the high slopes of the distant mountain. There was a rider up there, someone in buckskin, long as a dress . . . The rider turned the mount slowly and the familiar palomino with speckled rump heaved into a run and disappeared over the ridge, the rider's long hair flying . . .

Geary was saying something to him and he looked blank.

'Sorry — can't hear too well . . . '

'Was wonderin' why you were lookin' like that — kind of sad. You're not sorry about all them screamin' Injuns now lying dead, are you?'

Nolan smiled crookedly, shook his head.

'No. Truth is, I was thinking of those Injuns still living, the womenfolk in particular . . . '

'Well, you always were a strange one, Matt!'

Behind them a blood-spattered captain in soiled army tunic which was open, showing a bare white chest scarred by a knife-cut, came up, bloody sabre in hand. He glanced at Nolan and Geary, but spoke to Barney.

'Well, a successful mission. Cost some lives but *damned* successful. Congratulations, Lieutenant Wales.'

* * *

'I still don't see how you could've counted on Bob and me meeting up and then discussing our gold in your cell-block.'

The group was outside the Cheyenne courthouse now, awaiting the judge's verdict on Black Wolf and several of his warriors, on trial for treason and insurrection. Barney shook his head.

'Didn't count on it. I'd been workin' under cover for the army — there was a Gatling gun loose somewhere and it had to be found. The army never forgets. And I was in charge when the Gatling was stolen. Heard Bodie and McAlpine were in Arizona and that Black Wolf was plannin' an uprising. He had that stage act and I knew it figured in the deal somehow — I'm a man who follows his hunches. Turned out the act was only an excuse to travel around while they looked for Bodie and McAlpine — experts on Gatling guns and suppliers of rifles to anyone who could pay. Wolf didn't have much money, but then you showed up with your gold — and a yen for Abby. Pure luck for all concerned. 'Cept you maybe.'

'So you were acting out your role as a sheriff when you threw Bob and me in your brother's cells?' Nolan asked. 'Made up that story we'd killed Marney and his men. Just so you'd have an excuse to take us to Cheyenne.'

'Looked better that way, a lawman just doin' his job. Didn't want Wolf to think we might be on to him. That passageway in my cell-block was a fluke, the way it carried sound. And when I heard you two talking about Abby and Black Wolf and a heap of gold they'd stole from you . . . ' Barney spread his big hands. 'Had to follow through. Din' know whether you were involved for sure, but we knew you'd be going after Wolf. I stayed in the sheriff character, even stirred up my kid brother for extra effect — and — well, you know the rest.'

'A lot of damn luck involved!' said Geary. 'Matt and me might've give up on the gold and then you'd've had nothin'.'

'No, we knew Bodie and McAlpine were at Elk Mountain by then, showin' the Indians how to use repeating rifles and the Gatling gun. We'd been working on this thing for a long time. What we were waiting for was news of the attack, when it was due to happen. And where. You two with your blundering and plain ornery cussedness, set the cat among the pigeons there and — well, we only just managed to save the troop from total slaughter.'

'And for which the army is mighty grateful,' spoke up the captain.

'We get a reward?' Geary asked hopefully, but the officer merely smiled thinly.

'Just our undying gratitude.'

'Well, we can buy a horse ranch with *that!*' Geary said bitterly but the court orderly appeared and motioned them back inside. The verdict was about to be given.

The judge ordered Black Wolf and his six surviving warriors to be hanged forthwith on the Cheyenne gallows, and closed the court immediately.

Outside again, Barney Wales lost no time farewelling Nolan and Geary. No handshakes.

'Won't see you again, I guess, and don't want to. You're tough *hombres.* Now I better go make my peace with l'il brother — and his wife! Go back to Texas, you want my advice.'

'We don't even want that from you, Barney,' Nolan said quietly. 'Just get outta our lives.'

Wales laughed. 'Well, you've earned this much, I reckon.'

And to their surprise, Wales gave them a snappy salute before mounting and riding off.

As they unhitched their horses Geary

looked soberly at Nolan.

'What about Abby?' he asked.

'They haven't found her. One of the clerks said she took a strongbox with her, likely what was left of the gold.'

'Too bad. Treacherous bitch.'

Nolan shrugged. 'She's alone now, can't do much harm.' Geary sighed heavily. 'Well, wouldn't bet on that, the way she hates! Our luck's runnin' true to form, ain't it.'

'Aw, I dunno. There's always more gold. If you know where to look.'

Greary settled into leather.

'Think they'll ever find her?' he asked quietly.

Nolan shrugged. 'Don't care.'

'You wouldn't want to — go look?'

Nolan shook his head without hesitation.

'Nah. I made that mistake once and that's enough. C'mon, Bob. Let's go — there's nothing for us here.'

Geary glanced up, following Nolan's gaze to where the top bar of the new gallows showed beside the courthouse.

He saw a rope snake up and fall over the crossbar, followed by another and another ... seven in all. Soon they would stretch taut with the weight of the convulsing bodies of Wolf and his warriors ...

Bob Geary turned to his pardner who was just kicking his heels into his sorrel's flanks.

'You're right, Matt. There's nothin' here for us. Let's ride.'

THE END

We do hope that you have enjoyed reading this large print book.

Did you know that all of our titles are available for purchase?

We publish a wide range of high quality large print books including:
Romances, Mysteries, Classics
General Fiction
Non Fiction and Westerns

Special interest titles available in large print are:
The Little Oxford Dictionary
Music Book, Song Book
Hymn Book, Service Book

Also available from us courtesy of Oxford University Press:
Young Readers' Dictionary
(large print edition)
Young Readers' Thesaurus
(large print edition)

For further information or a free brochure, please contact us at:
Ulverscroft Large Print Books Ltd.,
The Green, Bradgate Road, Anstey,
Leicester, LE7 7FU, England.
Tel: (00 44) **0116 236 4325**
Fax: (00 44) **0116 234 0205**

Other titles in the
Linford Western Library:

ROPE JUSTICE

Ben Coady

Dan Brady is resting at a creek when, hearing a commotion on the opposite side of the water, he discovers a lynching in progress. Brady's sense of justice spurs him to prevent the lynching. But he finds he's pitched himself into a bitter feud. Now he is faced with a powerful rancher as his enemy, a crooked marshal, a bevy of hard cases and a gunfighter . . . A veteran of many tight spots, Brady might be making his final stand.

GOLD OF THE BAR 10

Boyd Cassidy

Gene Adams and his riders of the Bar 10 had brought in a herd of steers and been paid. Deciding to visit friends, Adams, Tomahawk, Johnny Puma and Red Hawke retrace an old trail on their way back to Texas. But an outlaw gang trails them, interested in the gold in Adams' saddlebags. And ahead of them two killers have kidnapped Johnny's sweetheart, Nancy . . . Can these legendary riders survive the dangers looming on all sides?

DAKOTA GUNS

Mike Stall

Jack Thorn had become a hunter after some of Quantrill's Raiders, under Captain Charlie Chiles, had killed his wife and child. Now, with only Chiles left, Thorn was trailing him towards the Dakotas. Here the Sioux were squaring up to Custer, and Thorn's old commander, General Hipman, was defending Fort Burr. But Chiles had a new line selling guns to the Sioux . . . If only Jack could track Chiles down, he would prevent the greatest disaster the West might ever know.

REDMAN RANGE

David Bingley

When he rode towards New Mexico territory, Rusty Redman expected to find the Redmans of Redman City friendly to a man with the same surname. His outlook changed, however, when he found Laura Burke fleeing from her Redman kin, fearing for her life, and witnessed Redman hirelings bullying farmers. In Big Bend, he took up arms against their gunslingers and played a highly dangerous part in bringing law and order back to the ordinary people.